NOTHING SOLD THE NEWS LIKE MURDER.

At last Carl could relax. He got out of his car. No passers-by.

The Lonely Hearts card came first; he tore it three times and threw it into the sewer. His balled, blood-stained handkerchief was next. The ring...*To Charlotte from John, with love*...He dropped it into the sewer.

When he turned into the alley behind the Garden, he could hear laughter. He lit a cigarette and entered.

"You got away with it, didn't you, boss?"

THE DARK PAGE

SAMUEL FULLER

AVON
PUBLISHERS OF BARD, CAMELOT, DISCUS AND FLARE BOOKS

AVON BOOKS
A division of
The Hearst Corporation
959 Eighth Avenue
New York, New York 10019

First Avon Printing, January, 1983

AVON TRADEMARK REG. U. S. PAT. OFF. AND IN
OTHER COUNTRIES, MARCA REGISTRADA, HECHO EN
U. S. A.

Printed in the U. S. A.

WFH 10   9   8   7   6   5   4   3   2   1

To my wife, Christa,
and our daughter,
Samantha

BOOK ONE

One

That night Carl Chapman touched greatness.

Tomorrow the headline would read: 12,000 MADE HAPPY!

Forty-eight booths surrounded the dance floor in Madison Square Garden, a pennant bearing the name of a state over each.

The place was jammed.

A buoyant Polish girl in a red sweater looked hopefully into the freshly shaved face of an employed truck driver, a Hungarian busboy-philosopher talked earnestly to a childless and restless Russian widow, a scrubbed washroom attendant with a Ghetto pallor simpered before an obese Cinderella, a baffled young German who could speak no English listened painfully to the high excited patter of a waitress, a gum-chewing Coney Island octogenarian was persuading a nervous school-teacher to share his interest in anthropology, bird calls and sex.

Romeos danced with Juliets who had their fingers crossed—dreamers, picketers, illiterates, first-paper citizens, optimistic clerks who talked bromides with passion, once-proud adventurers meek in the presence of middle-aged midwives who nursed vanishing dreams and growing regrets.

Hello, I am Glen . . . Hello, I am Pola . . . That blonde man is pretty . . . Look, he is looking at us . . . I am from a farm in Stor-Vindelsjo . . . Don't be bashful . . . That's a fine dress. I make dresses. I work in a factory . . . You dance fine, mister . . .

This was the Lonely Hearts Ball.

A sixty-foot banner was stretched across the far end of the arena; two huge hearts flanked the legend: COMET LONELY HEARTS CLUB.

Every one of the twelve thousand members wore a heart-shaped crimson card dangling from a red string attached to dress or buttonhole—and every card carried a year's subscription to the New York *Comet*.

There had been dozens of Get-Acquainted Clubs, Lonesome-Lovers Clubs, Companionship Clubs. But the *Comet* was the first newspaper to sell Love on a mass scale.

And it was Carl Chapman, *Comet* city editor, who gave birth to the idea, nursed it, made it grow to become newsdom's most ironic circulation booster.

In a corner near the Idaho booth he savored his own brainstorm. His eyes swept the crowd smugly. It represented dollars and cents, a jump in circulation and praise from his publisher. He had always known he had the talent, training and freakish love of shock to plan such a move; this charade would prove that throwing crumbs of romance to the love-starved paid off spectacularly. The mysteries, dangers, delights and promises discovered tonight would make every one of them a *Comet* reader for life.

A short swart woman was standing in front of him, grinning, her head coquettishly on one side. A thick gold brace held her large teeth in place. She was looking at him intently, waiting. She saw his official badge and turned away.

Then he saw his wife. She was dancing with a slight, slack-chinned man from Vermont. She was making him laugh. Rose had always been a good sport. That was one of the dozens of reasons he was so much in love with her. So closely attuned were they that she felt his presence across the milling couples. She turned, saw him and waved. He waved back.

A tiny figure cut across his line of vision—Julie Allison. She was so little, and her sincerity was so big; she was dashing back and forth making members comfortable, answering questions and thrilling to love blooming among strangers whose hearts were on their sleeves.

A tall, lanky young man pushed his way through the crowd, his blue eyes searching the faces impatiently. This was the first time that night Carl had seen Lancelot Seumas McCleary. He started to break through the lines to reach him.

A fat Swedish woman, her rouge applied in two blazing disks of orange-yellow, wearing a blue-velvet dress, fell in love with Lance McCleary a few feet away from the Indiana booth and blocked his way with a smile.

Carl ducked behind the booth.

"I am Hulda," he heard her say to Lance. "Fine party, yah?"

Carl chuckled. Lance had taken a step back from the beaming perfumed mountain that had suddenly risen in front of him.

"Yah," he muttered, a feeble mimic.

She leaned forward and read the card hanging from his buttonhole. "Number one-four-six-eight-six. *Blick!* See—I yahm two-three-nine. Old member. You yust yoin up, yah?" Before Lance could reply, she swung him out onto the crowded dance floor. Carl craned his neck to watch.

Two bars and the music stopped. Lance tore himself away and fled. But No. 239 was undaunted. The chase was on. Carl ran from behind the booth in time to see her hands coil around Lance's neck. The fugitive from love whirled.

"*Varsor springer?* Why you run?" she asked innocently, casually scrubbing the streak of brown grease which tattooed her elbow. "Don't be bashful, *vacker man*. Luffly boy, I like you. You like me, yah?"

She squeezed Lance's hand affectionately; he winced under the pressure. He desperately sought a way out as she whispered that they were soul mates. Her clutch on his arm compelled him to listen. There was nothing else for him to do, no escape whatever.

Carl decided Lance had had enough. He stepped forward, neatly divided them and bowed graciously to her.

"Pretty soon pictures," he told her musically. "Your picture in paper, yah?"

"Me? *Porträtt?*" she gasped.

Carl instructed her to wait near the North Carolina booth for the photographer, and promised he wouldn't lose sight of her new-found mate.

"Yah!" she said. Her eyes drank Lance in avidly. She stroked his cheek. *"Vacker man,"* she said, sing-song. Then she waddled away. Lance turned on Carl, now laughing uncontrollably.

"Look at it!" he said bitingly, snapping the card against his lapel with his finger. "Cute!"

Carl wiped the tears from his eyes.

Lance went on. "I fell for Julie's song-and-dance like a mugwump. You knew I would all the time. When I find that little—"

Carl smiled. Getting his top-notch crime reporter to the Lonely Hearts Ball had been easy, thanks to Julie and her warm eyes.

Lance glanced wryly at the heart pinned to him. "I must have lost my mind letting her drag me here. Well, boss, why the shanghai?"

"Calm down, Lance. Have some laughs."

"Like that beef-trust with a ton of powder! If you hadn't answered my SOS she'd have—"

"You can't blame her. Faint heart sleeps alone."

"All right, you had your laugh. What's it all about?"

"You're covering this tonight."

"Now *I'm* laughing. Getting me over here is one thing, making me write it is another."

"Anybody can write this yarn—but it needs *something*. You've got it."

Lance yawned. He looked the crowd over. "I'm going home. I like being lonely."

"Why do you think I got you over here—just to

look at you, you red-headed sourpuss? I got plenty of the boys covering this and they'll all give me the same old bushwaw—but what I want is the McCleary touch."

Lance's answer to that was short, to the point, profane.

"Who said you're going to win the Pulitzer Prize?" said Carl. "All you got to do is wander—the story will write itself."

"Another five minutes in this love-nest of slap-happy slobs and I'll break into tears!"

"That's what I mean. Tears and ink—nice gooey molasses."

Lance looked bored, a hopeful sign. When he got sour enough he'd write it, and the more sour, the more sentimental.

"Lance, there's nothing so pleasing to most tastes as a good mouthful of molasses. But not too thick. You hate this setup enough to make the story sing. And tears and ink will make any circulation jump." Carl placed a paternal arm about his charge. "What do you say, boy? Give Papa some nice molasses—a couple columns of it."

Strange, he thought, that he should be asking Lance instead of telling him. He knew all he had to say was "Write it!" and it would be written. But he understood Lance. It had been trying at first to guide this Irish protégé who was a writing fool; whose stories had been gaudy, swashbuckling, ranting, splashed with a dead-pan vehemence and a little sour cream of kindness. He had recognized in young McCleary, then a graduating copy boy, a natural newspaperman

—the type who could with training divorce himself from his story, study it coldly, digest it cynically, write it pointedly.

Lance shrugged. "All right, Papa," he said wearily, surveying the crowd. "I'll give you so much goo, you'll clog the presses with it."

Carl watched him disappear.

"Help! Mr. Chapman, help!"

He turned. Three hundred pounds of terror, box slung over his shoulder, was appealing to him. He was the *Comet* photographer, fat, genial Amos Biddle, ringed by a half-dozen women, his face perspiring through its fear. Never before had Carl seen Amos' huge figure cower. He neared the edge of the circle and heard the noisy Lonely Hearts bombard the cameraman.

"I am Pola Nogurski. I pose for picture again, no?"

"I like fat men."

"Please, my picture in paper tomorrow?"

Tomorrow. Tomorrow they would be out of circulation again, back to their pails and mops and aprons. For the second time that night he played hero. He broke through the ring and addressed Amos, his voice edged with sarcasm. "When you get through playing Casanova—" Amos' eyes bugged with desperate appeal. Carl turned to the women. "Go easy on him, ladies. He's tired, see? He's got work to do too."

They listened quietly, their eager eyes feasting on Amos' flushed face.

"*Let's go*, boss!" Amos charged through the women.

Carl consoled them with, "Later—more pictures for everybody."

He caught up with Amos who had paused near the Arizona booth to catch his breath.

"Thanks, boss!"

"Never mind that. Waste any plates?"

"Nah. Unloaded all the time."

"That's what you get kidding them you're taking their picture. Now get started on group shots of the Lonely Hearts in front of their home state booths."

"All forty-eight?" protested the lazy cameraman.

"Complaining?"

"No, no, boss. Forty-eight? Forty-eight."

"Right. Old sweethearts finding each other, new romances, triangles. Give me contrast."

Amos turned to leave when he was recalled and introduced to a Hungarian giant.

"This is Walther Zcekely," said Carl. "A setup. I'll announce the act later. Meanwhile grab plenty of stuff on him and his girl, Ilona—uh—"

"Mathusek," completed Zcekely hoarsely.

"There she is over there, grinning at us. Get them meeting as strangers at the Wisconsin booth. Show them dancing, discussing the old country, Uncle Sam, their second papers; show them reading the *Comet*, comparing club cards, falling in love, proposing, accepting and kissing."

"Great stuff, boss!" Amos was alive again. "Let's go, Romeo," he said leading the tzigane away. "We're going to get started on your true love story. You too, Ilona."

He motioned with both hands to the Lonely Hearts to line up in front of their booths, while assistants rushed about, echoing his orders.

Carl strode through the crowd. Near the platform he turned, eyes snapping as he plotted a fresh exploitation stunt. He caught sight of a healthy specimen of manhood standing a few feet away from him, and wondered if his figure was as well cut as the Michigan hunky's. He drew in his stomach self-consciously. Relaxed again, he rocked on his heels and toes, hands clasped behind him, admiring the army of *Comet* subscribers as Caesar admired the spoils following a victorious campaign.

He stood five feet eight inches in his stocking feet but preferred to measure his status by inches of newsprint and gains in the circulation field. Now in his forties, by his own standard, he grew wondrously tall. It would have been bad, he thought, if he hadn't been able to live up to the cocky assurance he had exhibited in those *Chronicle* days. That was how he was—different from all the others. He was born a rebel. He had never been content to be the best rewrite man on Park Row. Hadn't he seen what happened to faithful rewrites? To grizzly war-horses of the slot? To leg-men who suffered from varicose veins and reporters who dreaded the stomach pump?

Sure, top rewrite and all that wisdom about obedience . . . that the meek inherited the earth . . . but he knew that his boss was on his way home every night to a loyal wife and admiring children. He, too, wanted to issue orders from a swivel chair, own his own home and marry Rose. Sweet, lovely, golden-haired Rose with her shining eyes. Always frail. Always beautiful.

That night they went out . . . his fourth date with

her. She said he was spending too much, but his mind was on his career. Hobbyhorse for the editorial writer for two years! Wasn't he entitled to a break? He had great plans. That was why he had come to New York in the first place: to get a break, to get a fresh start.

"Where do you come from, Carl?" she asked as he spent his last dollar on wine. He rambled on, evading the question. He felt very low. . . .

The day the New York *Globe* was murdered, he was lifted into one of the big jobs of Manhattan journalism—the city editorship of the New York *Comet*, newcomer to the wayward press. To embark on something new proved simple for him, for he had a jungleful of ideas. He had a glorious, exciting, rip-snorting time adjusting himself to his new job, to his new life. He found a boisterous roughhousing staff and licked it into a fanatically loyal news machine by daily, hourly repetition of his favorite slogan, "Lots of socko!"

In the beginning the *Comet* had been a half-hearted challenge to the other papers, but his brains were the timely transfusion that saved its life. He had to battle envious desk-men over half-baked features. He tasted revolt, slammed his fist on the desk and bawled orders, terrifying them into submission. Men feared him, men respected him, and his worst foes conceded his capacity. But few loved him.

Headlines were big and bold, but not as big and bold as he saw them. He had no friends in those bitter days when he was king of the city room, his crown still glistening, a blue pencil in one hand and an aspirin tablet in the other—until he immortalized himself as a husband and father with, "I'M GLAD HE'S A GIRL, ROSE!" the headline-of-the-week.

The day Tommy was born he was promised a bonus for every hundred thousand increase he showed in the *Comet's* circulation. He worked hard, sat late at his desk, coat off, sleeves rolled up. . . .

His first love was the paper. His second, his home. But he had discovered the formula for complete contentment and never lost this harmony of desk and home. He guarded it jealously, prepared to defend it, ready to battle anyone who dared rob him of a precious part of it.

Life was complete to him.

Then he made rivals scratch their smug heads and whistle when he founded the *Comet* Lonely Hearts Club. Circulation mounted quickly, steadily. He became journalism's white-haired boy and recieved flattering offers from other publications. But he remained loyal to the *Comet*. He could afford to be loyal now.

And then he promoted the Lonely Hearts Ball.

The Garden was sold out. He smiled, rocking back and forth on heel and toe. Now he had everything. He had Rose, two lovely children, his swivel chair, his own home. He had reached his goal. He was The Great Editor. He was a devoted husband, a beloved father. He was the most contented man on earth.

Then he heard two words. Two words that threatened to strip him of his power, glory and happiness.

"John Grant!"

Two

Carl whirled about. He could see nothing but black eyes staring at him—strange, hypnotic, penetrating. There was something vaguely familiar and frightening about them. . . .

Take it easy. I'm just tired. Too much work before the ball. Just nerves, that's all. I checked. They told me she was dead. She's dead.

He took a step backward. An illusion?

The woman with the black eyes stepped forward. A reality.

Reality seized his wrist. "John, it's you. It *is* you!" The whisper came from a throat choked with tears. From the depths of her eyes came a plea for recognition. Her face was pale and alive. The alarming parade of years raced through his brain. She had been rosy-cheeked and pretty, not gaunt and tubercular.

"Charlotte!"

The word had shot out of his mouth before he could prevent it. Now it was too late for denial. Silence answered him. Her fingers dug into his flesh.

She was trying to speak. She found her voice again, thankful, shaking, low.

"John!"

People and booths and pennants and Biddle's flashes began to take form again to Carl. He looked around quickly. *I've got to get her out of here!*

No one was paying attention to them. He gripped her arm and pushed through the throng toward the rear exit leading out to the alley. Someone brushed past her and she stumbled. The button on Carl's sleeve tangled with the red string attached to her dress over her heart—the Lonely Hearts Club card. He freed his arm and pushed ahead.

They plunged into the alley. Air rushed into his lungs. He muttered a question and she mumbled an answer. Good; she didn't live far, just a half-dozen blocks down the street. He helped her into his coupe and drove off.

He needed gas. Funny, how you think of a silly thing like gas when you—

"That's it, John. The one with the light."

He stopped in front of a tenement, followed her stiffly up the cheap stairs—there seemed to be thousands. Outside a door on the second floor, she fumbled with her purse. The sound of a key in the lock and the opening of a door reached his ears in the dark. He felt her walk past him. She hesitated, groped in the inky blackness above her head and found the electric cord.

"Come in, John."

It was damp; a smell of medicine nauseated him.

She must be sick, he thought. He closed the door and turned slowly; walking as if he were in a nightmare to the lone window facing the dirty street, he drew down the patched shade as an elevated train stampeded past, arm's distance away. Her eyes did not leave him as he made a slow circle. At last he turned to look at her.

She was wearing a black dress greenish with age. She had put on a crisp white organdy collar and bow in a pathetic effort to look smart. He was glad that he could pity her and that pity could be so impersonal.

She misunderstood his silence.

"I—I've changed," she said apologetically. "Haven't I?"

What could he say? To him she was a skeleton in a closet he had locked, bolted, barred. He had thrown the key away, he had forgotten where. He had found contentment and peace in forgetting.

She was crying. Somehow tears had always become her. She swayed. For a moment he thought she was going to fall. He helped her to the bed and the snap of a spring reacted to her weight. He decided not to sit next to her. The bed wouldn't hold them both.

"Why, John? Why?" she asked in a whisper.

Tell her. Tell her. But he didn't. He felt her eyes devour him. She took his hands in hers and gently guided him down to the bed beside her. He studied her hands. They weren't smooth and pink as he remembered them; it was hard to believe they could be so bony and rough and dry.

A flood of memories overwhelmed him. How many

times had they sat together like this? For a moment anguish gripped him; he would have renounced his career and all he possessed to be twenty years younger enjoying a stroll with her near Holy Cross in Worcester.

You know you wouldn't, not for all the money in the world.

She withdrew her hands slowly. "The night you left me . . ." She held up her wrists so that he could see the scars that crossed them. "Oh, John, I'm so happy now that the doctor saved me. I didn't want to live then. I went away. I sold everything. Even those blue wine glasses you always liked. I washed dishes, clothes, floors—anything for money to keep on looking. I had to find you. I got in trouble, changed my name. Smith. Brown. Jones. It was terrible, John. I was lonely. Oh, so lonely! I had to find out why you ran off. I had a right to know. I must know."

"Charlotte, I'm married."

He felt her fingers grow cold. He got up and began a caged pacing. Then he told her—how he had changed his name to Carl Chapman, how he had struggled and dreamed and how he had met Rose and finally realized his ambition.

"I'm happy, Charlotte. You wouldn't know what that means. You never saw me happy. I have a home, a name, a future."

There, I told her. That's the way to do it. Right to the point. Get it over with. I'll manage her.

Finally she spoke. He strained to catch the word. "Married?"

He waited. She looked up slowly; eyes of pain met

his. The elevated roared by, vibrating through the room. She rose, steadying herself against the bedpost.

"What about me? *I'm* your wife."

No, Charlotte, you were never my wife. We stood up together and said words and you called me husband and I called you wife, but you were never my wife. You were too possessive. Always yours. Always yours. I was in a rut and you kept pulling me down. The more you liked me, the more I disliked you. The more you encouraged me, the less ambitious I became. You bored me. You irritated me. Your slightest touch nauseated me. I couldn't stand you another moment. I had to leave you. I had to drive you out of my life. No, Charlotte, you were never my *wife*.

He said, "Charlotte, I have two children."

"I don't care about them. You belong to *me!*"

Look at her. Still the same Charlotte. Selfish. Mine! Mine! Twenty years and no change. Hanging on. Hanging on.

"There was one thing I wouldn't pawn!"

She thrust out her left hand. The light above caught the band on her finger. The wedding ring winked at him. She seized his arms in a frantic grasp. "Why did you leave me, John? What did I do? You meant everything to me. I never hurt you. I loved you. I never stopped loving you."

He couldn't take his eyes from her haggard face. "You didn't get a divorce. You couldn't, John."

"They told me you were dead," he said.

But she was deaf to that. "We're married. We're married!"

"You were married to John Grant." There was a

savage sting to his words. "John Grant is dead. Everything connected with John Grant is dead. Everything. You must understand."

"Understand?" she cried. "You're still my husband. I've never given up hope of finding you. Understand? You should show a little understanding for your wife. For your *real* wife!"

She tugged at the Lonely Hearts card hanging over her heart. "Do you understand *this?* Do you understand the hell I've been through; how low I've fallen to seek companionship in a club—in a lonely hearts club—in *your* club?"

The three words choked her. She coughed and he turned his eyes away, shivering, pitying her. He had to stop this. He straightened with a gesture of finality. "Charlotte, I love my wife. I love my family. Nothing can make me give them up. Nothing. We must be sensible."

"Sensible! We took an oath. ' 'Till death do us part.' You deserted me! Do you call that sensible? I want my chance now. I deserve it."

He became aware of a change in the temper of his thoughts. His pity for her was swept aside by impatience.

"I have money, Charlotte . . ."

She was kissing his hands.

" . . . you can go away. I know a doctor in Bermuda who will—"

She sprang away. Her eyes glared and her voice was a sword swinging. "You cheat! You fraud! You liar!"

"Charlotte!"

"I'll tell them. I'll tell them who you really are.

I'll tell them about the woman you're living with! I'll tell . . . I'll tell . . . I'll tell . . ."

Crazed by her own hysteria she rushed toward the door, flung it open. He pulled her back and slammed it shut.

Again she came on. "I'll tell!" She flung herself on the door. He tore her hand from the knob, seized her by the shoulder and pushed her away violently.

The crashing roar of a passing elevated filled the room . . . She clutched his coat. Her ringed fist missed his face. In him he felt the passions of a stranger, a man he didn't know, and his fist struck the side of her head. She fell backward with a howl of terror.

His mouth was acid; he had lost his tongue. There was an empty silence in the room as he tried to cry her name.

She was on the floor, motionless.

A pain shot through his head. He saw himself striking her and buried his head in trembling hands, but the picture raced before him in his mind, vivid, horrifying. He had struck her again and again, no longer trying merely to keep her from the door or from exposing him; trying only to destroy her.

Again he cried her name and again there was silence and she was still on the floor, motionless, her head against the iron foot of the bed. He bent over her.

Fear and relief swept him. He placed his hand behind her head and withdrew it red. . . .

Footsteps! Was someone coming up the stairs? Had

anyone overheard? They're passing. They're stopping. No, they're going on.

He was still crouching. Panic seized him. *I've got to get out of here!* But his feet had grown to the floor; he could not move. . . . Only his hands were mobile. With his handkerchief one was wiping the blood from the fingers of the other, carefully, one by one. They were the hands of a stranger.

Their action released him. He was Carl Chapman! Carl Chapman had nothing to fear, there was nothing Carl Chapman could not do! He had but to think . . . *to think* . . .

He forced himself to look at the body. Once again panic: *Run! Get out. Get out.* He drove it back.

His eyes went about the room, inch by inch; he saw it in its minutest detail . . . He must rehearse every step, every particular—then he would act.

The ticking of his watch was loud in his ears. He had a sense of time rushing by him. *Hurry! Hurry!* Still he stood. . . .

Now!

Her purse—he opened it: a compact, a change purse with three pennies, a quarter and the key to the room, a crumpled package of cigarettes and a book of matches, a lipstick, a comb, a want-ad clipping, a soiled handkerchief, and a pawn ticket. He put that too in his pocket.

He went through the bureau drawers starting at the top, searching each one quickly, thoroughly, replacing each article.

I changed my name, had to. Smith. Brown. Jones. Good. She'd be unidentified.

The last drawer stuck. He pulled at it, shaking it, pushing it up, down. Unreasoning fury shot through him. Was he to be held up by this? He drew out the drawer above it, thrust his fist through and banged the bottom one open. There was nothing in it.

The closet—bare; the improvised kitchenette; under the bed . . . no suitcase anywhere.

He turned down the bed, picked up a love story magazine from the floor. Run-down slippers were there. He must remember them. The magazine and the cigarettes and matches from the purse went on the table beside the bed.

The slippers . . . he carried them into the bath-room, cursing the precious second it took him to find the light cord. A nightgown and an ancient bathrobe were hooked on the door. He draped them over the bathroom chair, placed the slippers near it. He folded a used bathtowel and hung it over the tub-rack. Soap . . . Washcloth . . . Powder . . . Bath salts . . . no bath salts.

He plugged the tub drain with the stopper and turned on the tap. Warm water trickled sluggishly.

He stood by the body. Blood! What about the blood? He knelt and lifted the head. The bruise was dry. Basal fracture. Clot. Lucky . . . But the iron foot of the bed was stained. He moistened a corner of his handkerchief and rubbed the stain away.

Now he was ready . . . The wedding ring slipped off easily, she was so thin; she had had to wind a string around it to keep it on. He pulled off her shoes and flung them across the floor as if she had kicked them off tired feet.

Then he stripped the body.

He stood up. Breathing was difficult. He waited deliberately until his hands stopped trembling and he could swallow.

He found a split hanger in the closet, slipped the dress over it and hung it on the open closet door. He took stockings and underwear to the kitchenette sink, drenched them, wrung them out, spread them over the cord stretched from corner to corner.

Now the last step. . . .

He had rehearsed this so stonily in his mind, so perfectly. But he was paralyzed, fighting the horror that welled up in him until he wanted to disgorge.

Come on. You were a police reporter once. You covered the morgue. You saw them—so many of them—all kinds. You can't stop now. You can't! *Move!*

He bent over, hooked his hands under the shoulders and dragged the body into the bathroom.

The tub was filling. He lifted the legs and let them drop over the rim of it. He was panting now. Straining every muscle, he lifted the body to a standing position in the tub.

Its knees buckled. A foot slipped and the body sagged. For an instant he thought everything was lost. He had to struggle to keep his balance. He set his teeth.

Slowly, measuring the distance, he allowed the feet to slide toward the end of the tub. Enough! His heart beat thickly in his throat as he used all his strength to hold the body up. It must be at an angle, its back to the faucets, its head directly over them. That was it. The bruise must be directly over the faucets.

A moment to steady himself . . . He sprang back.

The body dropped. The back of its head struck both faucets with a thud. Its arms flew up. One foot waved crazily and came down with a splash.

The flying water spattered the wall, nightgown and robe, dumped the can of talc and filled one of the bedroom slippers. He escaped it.

He tiptoed in, avoiding the puddles on the floor and set the soap down in one of them.

He was finished. It was done.

Back in the bedroom, he straightened his jacket, ran his hands over his hair. Only the continuing purl of water and his own breathing made sound in the apartment.

Now he was in a fever to be gone. He opened the door, glanced up and down the dark hallway. He turned to take one last careful look. He must be sure.

A flash of bright red leaped to his eyes. The Lonely Hearts Club card! His pulse hammered. If he had forgotten it!

He crossed swiftly to the dress on the closet door, tore the card from it, and went out. As he closed the door, the shattering roar of a passing train came to him for the last time.

Three

The street was empty. Two quick strides took him to the coupe. He drove off.

He counted the blocks and pulled up to the curb. There was more he must do. But he had to wait. He locked his teeth against nausea and bowed over the wheel, forehead hard against it, hands clenched around it. Chill after chill shook him.

At last he could relax. At last he could sit up. And with returning warmth and sanity, he felt a sort of triumph. Now there would be no more faltering.

He had stopped close to a sewer. He got out. No passers-by.

The Lonely Hearts card came first; he tore it three times and threw it into the sewer. His balled, blood-stained handkerchief was next. The ring . . . *To Charlotte from John, with love* . . . He dropped it into the sewer.

What else? There remained only the pawn ticket. He hesitated, replaced it in his pocket . . .

When he turned into the alley behind the Garden, he could hear laughter, excited voices, a steady hum of happiness. He lit a cigarette and entered.

Had anyone noticed his absence? *How long had he been gone?*

"You got away with it, didn't you, boss?"

Carl turned slowly. Amos Biddle grinned at him.

"If *I* was running this circus," said the cameraman, "*I'd* sneak out for some air, too."

Remember, you're still editor. Be one! "You'll get plenty of air if you don't hop on it. How much did you get?"

"Everything. Even a shot of that old guy from Frisco when he passed out. Excitement got him."

"Oh, yes. Change it to love. Build him up a hermit. Never thought he'd get a mate. Found one and passed out from the strain."

"And the lucky lady?"

"Hm—use that one over there—near Vermont. She's the type. Throw them together for a two-column."

"Anything else?"

"Yes. Lance still here?"

"You bet. You got to give Julie credit."

Carl pushed his way through to the center of the dance floor. From the platform he flagged for attention and announced one of the features of the evening, the Virginia Reel.

He called the changes. "Do-see-do, down the middle and back again." *Is my voice trembling?* "Swing your partner around to the right."

Why did you leave me, John?

"Swing your partner around to the right. Down the middle and back again. Swing your partner around to the right."

Square-jawed males and barrel-chested females, baldish waiters and big-boned wetnurses, paunchy men in hand-pressed suits and hoarse women who wouldn't gargle, clapped hands in time to *Turkey in the Straw, Dixie,* and *Yankee Doodle.* Soon a half-dozen reels, more energetic than polished, were in progress in different parts of the Garden.

Did I wipe the blood off the foot of the bed? Stop trembling. Raise your voice. Louder. That's too loud, too hysterical. Lower it. That's better.

The Virginia Reel completed, he raised his hands; the drummer rolled for silence.

Carl introduced the blushing Walther Zcekely and Ilona Mathusek, and announced the surprise engagement of the happy couple who had met at the Wisconsin booth.

"Strangers yesterday," he stressed dramatically. "Lovers tonight."

Amos Biddle winked and Lance McCleary yawned, but Julie Allison listened wide-eyed and thrilled to Carl's inspiring words as he addressed the eager faces turned up to him—their champion.

"They say I am the man who made the Lonely Hearts Club." *You just killed a Lonely Heart.* "It is not I. It is you out there who made this beautiful dream come true. Remember, you are here because you want someone to share your troubles and happiness. You are here to recognize Love."

Why did you leave me, John? I never stopped loving you.

"The *Comet*—I—we are interested in you men and women, in your welfare, your future. And what is a future? A future is a home. A future is the holiness prescribed by God that binds man to woman. A future is the wedding ring."

There was one thing I wouldn't pawn!

"I understand your trials and tribulations. I, too, know what it is to be lonely."

It was terrible, John! I was lonely. Oh, so lonely!

"I, too, suffered. For years my one ambition has been to wipe out the word lonely from our daily lives. I want every member who has walked the narrow corridor of loneliness to understand that the *Comet* is eager to help you find yourself . . . Companionship is the only tonic for lonesome men and women."

. . . how low I've fallen to seek companionship in a club—in a lonely hearts club—in your club?

He held up the heart-shaped emblem which each wore so proudly. "This is not just a valentine card. This signifies happiness, understanding, companionship, love.

"Because Walther met Ilona here they should be proud. They are proud.

"Walther is honest, sturdy, ambitious. He wanted a wife. Now he has found one and next week they will be married."

We're married. We're married!

"Walther—Ilona—when you stand up and take your oath to be true and faithful to each other until death, you are doing the most wonderful thing on earth."

" 'Til death do us part." You deserted me! . .

"The wedding ring—"

You cheat!

"—is the sacred bond—"

You fraud!

"—between man and woman!"

You liar!

A wave of encouragement and happiness swept over the Lonely Hearts. Their ovation was dramatic and thunderous.

And Carl Chapman was sick and cold. His ears rang and the lights blinded him and the flapping hands applauding him made him feel faint.

Then his curbing mind came to his support and things began to take shape again. He tingled, remembering, as he bowed gratefully.

For John Grant was dead, buried now forever.

Four

It was early morning. The garden was cool and quiet. He ached with weariness, his eyes dragged with it. But these were his moments alone in the garden he had created and he would not give them up.

Here was peace, here was sanctuary. Here he was himself. Here that other feverish world did not exist. Here was where he belonged. On his knees before a bush, he worked humus into the loam around the roots with scrupulous thoroughness. No part of his task bored him. He loved it.

The Chapman cat darted from behind the bush, slapping at a fly. She arched her back and rubbed against him, kneading rhythmic paws into the humus bag. He pushed her away gently with the back of his hand. There was a patch of grass newly dried by the sun. She dropped to her back and rolled in it ecstatically, nipping at stray leaves. He caught himself wishing he could do that too.

Behind him was the white-frame house. He knew every inch of it. Its blue shutters . . . How Rose had laughed at him when he insisted on them. "Carl Chapman—old-fashioned!" Sheepishly he had tried to explain that to him they meant being able to shut out the rest of the world; and she had laughed again, indulgently, and kissed him.

They were never closed, but looking at them he felt an inarticulate deep content. Even in his youth he had never dreamed of turreted castles on river bluffs, or longed to own a luxurious houseboat. This was what he wanted, this was what he had achieved. His home—the center of the earth—and all heaven was snug within it.

This was happiness.

He moved to the next bush, measured humus expertly. It had all been raw earth. But he had dug deep, planting, spading, raking. Things grew for him. He had the "green hands."

He scooped up a handful of earth, crushed it, let it trickle through his fingers and felt the essence of his importance. With these hands he made things grow out of the earth.

With these hands you killed.

He recoiled. His breath sucked in and he was weak. He tried to rise and flee from horror but he could not. In his ears there was the roaring of a passing elevated train. He saw a man striking a woman, saw her fall, saw the look of triumph and relief on the man's face.

I have killed.

He had felt no remorse. He was not sorry she was dead. He was glad!

He rocked back and forth, screaming without a sound. But he had not moved. He was pinned to the earth, defenseless, gasping and blind. He had killed and this was his punishment. Some mercy had kept judgment from him until now. But now he knew. He was guilty and every day punishment would return. All the rest of his life he would carry it with him . . .

He straightened. He held up his hands and studied them dully . . . He saw the humus bag again and the bush and the garden he had created. He turned and looked at his home and his garden. Peace and contentment . . . It was all strange to him. This too, then, was part of his punishment . . .

Cold hatred grew in him. *She* would like to see him punished. But he would not be. He took a step forward. I will not let this happen! Guilty? No—my will shall blot that out. Punishment? No—my will shall sweep that away. I can do it. I'm strong, strong . . . Nothing can touch me—nothing!

From an open window came Rose's laugh. The children were getting up. He could hear their high-pitched chatter.

As on every morning, Tommy was the first to come dashing out of the house. He stopped within a few feet of his father, clasped his hands behind his back and came forward, stiff-legged.

"Good morning, Mr. Whiffenpoof," he piped.

Carl looked down at him without a smile. This too was part of the ritual.

My son . . . Rose's eyes but my mouth and chin.

"Good morning, Mr. Kaflopsky, I see you have new overalls."

"On account of I'm a working man. I want two pounds of oranges, please."

Carl pretended to survey a crowded market. "Sorry, I'm fresh out of oranges. How about two nice bunches of radishes?"

Tommy giggled. "I can't buy them. My mother won't allow me." He found that very funny. With a shout, he flung himself on his father.

His daughter Edith flew down the path shrieking, "Me too! Me too!"

She was as light as a bird, the picture of Rose but with his own quick temper, his own greed for life. He hugged her convulsively. I'll give you everything— everything . . .

The children drew away and stood side by side looking up at him with sly shining eyes.

"There's a package in the hall," said Tommy.

"There *is?*"

Edith quivered with excitement. "Is it for you, Daddy?"

"No."

"For Mommy?"

"Not this time."

They were both dancing up and down, loving the suspense. "For the house?"

"No."

"For us?" they screamed together.

Carl nodded. They rushed off into the house and returned carrying the package between them. Their impatient fingers were ineffectual and fumbling. He helped them with the wrappings. They stared awestruck at the train in the box.

Edith tugged at the engine. "It's red!" she babbled. "Look, Tommy, it's red!"

But Tommy's eyes were on the ground. His lower lip was out and he had paled.

What was wrong? Yesterday Rose had said something about a fever. Carl put his hand to the child's forehead. "What's the matter?"

Tommy shook his head and pointed to the engine. Then he wasn't feeling ill. Carl squatted so he could look directly into his son's eyes and held out his hands. In immediate imitation, Edith squatted beside him peering up at her brother.

"What is it, son? You know you can tell me . . ."

"You said Sannaclaus was bringin' me a train for Christmas."

"Yes?"

"*You* brought it. He'll be mad. He won't bring me nothin'!" Tears were close.

Don't cry, my son. Don't let me ever be the cause for tears even such as these. "But didn't I tell you?" said Carl. "I wrote him a letter first. It's all right. He's bringing you something else."

Tommy's nose was less than two inches from his own. "What?"

Carl rose. "Oh, no you don't! Not until Christmas."

He watched them fall on the train, become instantly absorbed in its details.

"Carl Chapman, you're spoiling those children."

Rose had come up behind him, trying to look severe. He fitted her into the circle of his arm.

Now it was complete.

He felt his love grow into the earth, stretch into

the sky. It made a wall around them through which only he had the secret of entrance.

The three were looking at him, laughing. He knew the fierce joy of their dependence on him. This, all this, was his: always—forever.

Five

Lance McCleary reached for a ham sandwich and squinted disgustedly at the bold type across the front page as if he hated to admit it fully into his sight.

12,000 MADE HAPPY AT
COMET LONELY HEARTS BALL

Wisconsin Couple To Wed

"Tchah!" he said.

The fat police sergeant leaned over and picked up the paper, his stomach bulging over his belt with relief from the restraint of brass buttons. He read the headline.

"Now that's a damned good story."

Lance yawned. "You're a sentimentalist, Sarge." He brooded over his sandwich and cup of warm coffee. "A circulation stunt and you fall for it at your age."

Three cops were writing reports at the table in the muster room; in a corner one was having his shoes shined; two were studying the bulletin board; a duo were struggling through poker. They all grinned.

The sergeant reddened around the ears. "You got

the wrong attitude, Lance. You're cynical." He seemed proud of that one.

He read the account of the ball. He sighed. "Who wrote this, Lance?"

"Dunno."

"It hits home."

"Ugh!"

"Well, it's *your* paper."

"And it's the bunk."

The opening door let in the angry yell of a small boy being hauled in by a solicitous officer.

"I ain't lost!" roared the boy. "I'm runnin' away!" He made a lunge for the door, was recaptured. "He won't tell me his name," said the officer holding him.

"An' I ain't gonna tell you where I live neither!"

Sergeant Pike didn't look up from the Lonely Hearts story. "I know him," he said casually. "Met his ma a short while ago. Said she didn't want to see him again."

"That's right," said Lance indifferently. "I just left his father. *He* said he's glad his son ran away."

Anxious brown eyes went from face to face looking for a sign of contradiction, found none. The boy opened his mouth and howled; a flood of tears rolled down his cheeks. Blubbering incoherently that he wanted to go home, he was led out of the room.

The triple-chinned sergeant looked at Lance as if he expected something. He said: "I remember the day when you went for a kid story like that. Used to call it human interest."

Lance disposed his length more comfortably on

three chairs and took another bite of his sandwich. "Them days is gone forever," he sang through it.

"They sure is—are—You've changed, Lance."

"Yeah," put in the cop at the stand, "if the place isn't swimming in blood and there aren't more than ninety-three suspects, it's no story to Charlie Chan there."

One of the men at the table, paring his nails with a Boy Scout knife, grinned. "Don't you know?" he said. "He's a criminologist-reporter. *Time* Magazine said so."

Lance made a sour face, but he was pleased.

Only twenty-eight and criminologist-reporter . . . a far cry from that fresh kid with his first stiff police card, yellow and shiny and autographed by the Commissioner himself. He saw that lanky, clear-skinned cub as though it weren't himself: a kid who could leap on a riot truck as it rolled to an emergency and sit up all night writing and rewriting the special feature that was lost in page nineteen; who could spend eight hours in the rain with the sea-cops running down a junky smuggling alcohol and dope near Execution Light; who was thrilled when veteran newspapermen first called him Lance.

He slid lower on his spine and scratched his shoulder blades lazily against the back of the chair. He recalled every word in the *Time* article. "The thrill of the hunt is all that matters to tapered bloodhound Lance (*Comet*) McCleary who solved the grisly Leonard murder mystery (*Time*, Aug. 12, p. 31). His psychic deductions (i.e., hunches) were rare high points in the dramatic complexities which confused police. Now he (upped to criminologist-reporter) lies in wait for more baffling murder knots to untie. Newshawks envy his uncanny ability of carrying a fistful of clues in one hand, an impatient typewriter in the other (also his wages) ."

He smiled fondly at Sergeant Pike; the lovable bulk in blue had seen the kid that was Lance fervently poring over the mysteries of the police blotter and out of the kindness of his heart had made them intelligible to him.

Lance carefully stripped a piece of fat from the ham and flipped it into a wastebasket. He loved all mankind.

Then his eye fell on the *Comet* and he frowned. Of all papers!

But there were compensations. One was Carl Chapman.

He remembered, warmly, how Carl had hammered at him, ripped into his copy before the staff, taught him when to soften his satire, sharpen his adjectives, quicken his pace and sparkle more inventively, humorously and humanely. He loved Carl. He respected him. He was in debt to him. He wasn't working for the *Comet*. He was working for Carl Chapman.

Then there were other compensations—one hundred and five of them on a check every week. And a free hand with his crime stories.

He felt very virtuous this bright and sunny morning in the muster room barred to the public eye, where a small fraction of New York's finest let their hair down, cracked off-color jokes, gossiped and roughhoused. He had nothing to do but wait around until a big story broke. Easy pickings, this special feature stint. If Carl needed him, he knew where to reach him.

He was sipping his cold coffee, trying to imagine it had just been made, when the door creaked and opened slightly.

"Are you decent?"

Lance recognized the voice; he watched its effect on the cops. Sore feet moved quickly as the arm of the law sprang into action. They climbed into harness, forgot poker, shined shields. Sergeant Pike fastened his belt and called out dulcetly, "Come on in, Julie."

Without turning, Lance could picture her—as big as a minute, her black hair curling up around the funny little hat she wore pulled down over one shining blue eye, with a figure that rightfully belonged behind footlights and not behind a daily excerpt from the Bible.

In three years she had come a long way. She was now, if you please, Religious Editor of the *Comet*. He chuckled. What a job. And on the *Comet*. Incredible.

Abruptly, the sandwich was plucked out of his hand. He turned and stared up at her.

"*Mr.* McCleary!" Her chin elevated slightly. "Meat —on *Friday!*"

"Th' haythin," muttered a cop sympathetically.

It amused Lance to pretend to be sorry, so he said it to please her. "I'm sorry, honey, I forgot." She was wearing a black and white suit. "Golly, you look cute," he added.

She put her hands in the pockets of her jacket and

laughed, forgiving him, wrinkling her short eager nose.

"Mr. McCleary, that was a beautiful story." Before he could stop her, she turned to the cops. "Did you read the Lonely Hearts story he wrote?"

"Who wrote?" boomed Sergeant Pike, his eyes dancing.

"She's feverish," said Lance lightly. "Come on, Julie, I want to talk to you outside."

"Wait a minute," said the sergeant. "I want to congratulate you, Mr. Heart-of-Gold."

Julie's eyes widened. "Mr. McCleary tries so to be hard-boiled, but anyone could tell he wrote it even if he didn't want his by-line on it."

Lance looked at the cops and threw out his hands. "All right. All right. So I wrote it."

"You don't have to be modest, Mr. McCleary," said Julie. "It's the most wonderful—"

Lance laughed. For three years he had been unsuccessfully trying to get her to call him Lance, yet she persisted in this ridiculous formality for no reason he could discover.

"What are you thinking about?"

"Oh, maybe about your funny Irish nose," he said.

She smiled. What a girl—perfect! Some lucky guy will get her.

But she wanted *him*. Ah, no, Julie; I've seen what happened to reporters when they get married . . . kids, bills, diapers, bills, crazy hours, bills, crazy assignments . . . And anyway who wants to get married—yet?

"What brought you here?" he asked.

"Oh, I just dropped in to see the boys."

"You've seen them! Now come on, what's it all about?"

"Mr. McCleary"—she began with apprehension, finished determinedly—"I've come to ask you to do me a favor."

He was a chip from a tough, knotty Irish oak block. He could only be patient when a situation didn't concern him, endanger his freedom, or encroach on his sense of humor. Now he lost it.

"What?" he yelled. "Again?"

She lowered dark lashes. He changed his tone. "What is it?"

"Mabel's shower," she said softly.

Even the cops were stunned.

"She's getting married next Sunday and we girls are all bringing our boy friend—"

"Julie—for Pete's sake!"

But she went on "—and you've got to bring a present too!"

Lance glared. Then he realized all this was ridiculous. All he had to say was no.

"Some other time, Julie."

But she just stood there looking up at him without a word. Starting early in the morning, was she? Smart girl. No matter what kind of a fence he threw up around himself, he knew she'd work her way through it by the end of the day. He had to get out of here before those eyes began to wear him down again.

"Got to beat it, Julie," he said as if he just remembered he left his apartment in flames. "Got to run down a lead. Got to hurry. See you some more!"

She stepped in his way. "And Mabel's shower?"

"Oh—that!" He was careless, light, manufacturing a shrug. "We'll talk about it later."

"That's what they're doing," said a new voice. "Talking."

Amos Biddle, camera slung over back, shuffled into the muster room.

He smacked his lips over a bulging candy. "Your tear-jerker on Lonely Hearts made the rounds, Lance," he drawled. "The boys on Park Row are tearing down Civic Virtue. They're putting up a statue of you instead, with a broken heart in one hand and a roll of adhesive tape in the other."

The cops roared. Julie didn't think it was so funny and said so; but Lance saw in Amos Biddle a way out of her clutches.

"What are you doing here, Amos?" he asked amiably.

The cameraman was puzzled. He had expected an explosion. "I live down the block," he explained, still wary. "Had a hunch you'd be here." He shifted the candy. "Just dropped in to pat you on the back for the best slush I couldn't wade through."

"What's the box for?"

"Nothing that would interest you. The desk knew I had a Graflex home and as long as she was killed around here I could grab a coupla shots of her for—"

"Killed? Who was killed?"

"Forget it, Philo Vance. This dame is no news."

"You just said she was killed."

"Yup."

"And with that lead you call it no news?"

"No name."

"Names make news is okay," said Lance. "But not all the time." He took Amos' arm. "Let's go!"

"You're wasting your time, sucker. She's a nobody. She's out of your class."

" 'Or walk with Kings—nor lose the common touch.' Kipling," said Sergeant Pike solemnly.

As one, they turned and gazed at him, awed. "Just bought the poem for my boy," he muttered uncomfortably.

Lance picked up where he had left off. "Listen, Roly-Poly, I'll show you how to take a lead and make it sensational."

Amos laughed. "You think you can ring the bell just because she was killed and you got an imagination."

"What you got says I can't?"

"Five bucks says you can't."

"It's a bet. Get that boys? Witnesses. Don't let this guy crawl out when I win."

"But Mr. McCleary," broke in Julie, "how about—"

Lance dragged Amos to the door. "Come on, blubbermouth! Here's where I make me five bucks!"

The door slammed.

Sergeant Pike sat down in his chair and leaned back. "Great guy, Lance," he said fondly.

Suddenly his face dropped. *"Woman killed?"*

He leaped to his feet. "Hey, Lance!" he cried, lumbering to the door and wrenching it open. "Hey —*who* was killed? When? Where? How? *Hey!"*

Six

The morgue hearse parked in front of a tenement was the first thing Lance saw as he swung around the corner, the puffing Amos behind him. A cop shooing curious kids away greeted him.

"What are *you* doing here, Lance? Going to solve a mystery?"

Lance grinned. "First I got to collect five bucks, Eddie."

The cop shrugged. All reporters were crazy.

Amos pushed forward, a tank, making a hole through the people massing the entrance; Lance kept right behind him. The hallway was jammed with more of them: a woman holding a squalling brat, a rat-faced man staring, a sleepy streetwalker . . . And water on the stairs . . .

Amos climbed, breaking trail up the stairway. Lance followed him. The babble followed Lance:

"Who killed her? . . . She was stabbed . . . No, *shot!* I heard it . . . You heard nothin', Joe . . . Awshuttup! . . . Who is it? . . . I just seen her yestiday . . . She was lookin' for a job . . . Choked! Somebody choked her . . ."

The janitor's scrawny wife was sulkily mopping the wet floor in front of an open doorway. A cop blocked the path. Lance knew him.

"H'lo, Paddy."

The cop blinked. "We'll have to get the D.A. over now that Joe Hawkshaw's here." He jerked his head toward the room. "One of your girl friends, Lance?"

"Blonde?"

"No."

"She isn't."

Lance turned to Amos. "If you got it in one bill it'll be easier for you to count." He entered the room. The cop had to move for Amos.

Lance's first impression was a hunch—the janitor, on his knees in a corner of the squalid one-room apartment, soaking up water from the floor with dirty rags and wringing them out into a pail.

Lance didn't like it; he didn't like to walk into a story and see a janitor messing around. He shrugged. He had no time for hunches. This was just a casual drop-in, look-see and the collection of five dollars from an unimaginative cameraman. There was no reason for the vague uneasiness the janitor's grumbling gave him: "Water upstairs, downstairs, three hun'red sixty-four nights th' guy downstairs stays home. This one night he's gotta be out cattin'."

In the corner an assistant medical examiner was bent over a corpse on the bed. Lance remembered him. Dr. Kuppenheimer. A pain—gabby but uninformative; the type who always reads columns for the jokes he can memorize.

Dr. Kuppenheimer looked up. "Oh, McCleary. Slumming?"

Then he forgot Lance and continued his examination. Lance nodded to the cop on duty and to the police photographer, who was setting up his camera. He leaned over the iron railing of the bed casually.

"Fix the time, Doc?" he asked.

"If it'll help you get a raise—sometime last night."

"Hm." Lance rubbed his chin thoughtfully. The examiner glanced up, shook his head quizzically, and went back to the cadaver, his fingers swift, sure.

"Married?" asked Lance.

"Umph."

"Who killed her?"

"Umph."

"D'ya mind, buddy?" The janitor, on his knees, looked up impatiently, banging the pail against Lance's leg. "I wanna get over here."

Lance moved away. Funny, water all over the room. He heard the janitor muttering again: "Ain't got 'nuff work . . . damn dames gotta leave their water runnin' . . ."

Lance lit a cigarette. Investigation going on and they permitted a janitor in the room. There was a laxity present he didn't relish.

"I'm all set, Dr. Kuppenheimer," said the police photographer.

The man from the morgue motioned to the cop. Together they lifted the body and laid it on a sheet spread on the damp floor. Close-ups of the bruise on the head; repeated shots of front, back and profiles.

Lance was bored. Routine stuff. A stooge from the morgue, a cop who should be back at his school-crossing corner and a police photographer who couldn't make the grade with that news service outfit.

Finished, the photographer turned to Amos in the doorway. "What are you doing here, Biddle?"

Amos grunted. That was the second thing Lance didn't like. Amos was looking at him too lamblike. He should be in anguish, mopping his brow, losing some of that fat at the thought of parting with five dollars.

As Dr. Kuppenheimer knelt to make a closer examination of the head, Lance's eyes swept the room. Underwear and stockings hanging across a cord from corner to corner attracted his attention.

"She must have got it after she washed her clothes," he announced as if he had stumbled on an important revelation.

He circled the room slowly, eyes narrowed, chin out à la Sherlock Holmes, until his face unexpectedly ran into the cop's on duty.

"I read *Time* too," said the cop unemotionally.

Lance ignored him. He, too, knelt. "Bullet?"

Dr. Kuppenheimer shrugged.

Lance bent closer to get a better look. "Death blow, eh, Doc?"

Dr. Kuppenheimer ran his fingers over the left leg of the corpse. He moved around the body. Lance was in his way. "Maybe you want to make the report, Lance?"

Lance grinned, drew back. "Garrotted?"

No answer. Dr. Kuppenheimer kept on with his

work. Lance bit his lip. He didn't like him, either. He came close to the body again, walking on his knees, undaunted. "Lead pipe?"

Dr. Kuppenheimer looked thoughtful. "Lead? Maybe. . . . It's in the bathroom."

That was more like it! Lance sprang up and went to the bathroom, eagle-eyed.

"Look out!"

He stopped cold. The cop walked up to him. "You almost stepped on the soap," he said solicitously.

Always kidding around, these bulls. Lance stepped over the soap.

A moment later he hurried out. "Hey, Doc! I can't find it."

"Find *what?*"

"The—whatever she was struck with."

Dr. Kuppenheimer sat back on his heels. "Lance, are you drunk?"

Lance exploded. "Listen, Doc, I'm not here to play straight man. I'm in a hurry. How about a little cooperation?"

The examiner pursed his lips, waved his hand wearily, and turning to the cop, began, "Corpse marked—"

The cop laboriously took down the dictated report in his notebook. Lance gave up. He went over to the window and stared down at the kids hovering around the morgue wagon. Now he'd have to wait until that pompous butcher had finished rattling off.

"—tentative diagnosis," the examiner was continuing monotonously. "Impression is possible fracture of base of skull or subarachnoid hemorrhage—"

Lance lost his patience. "For the love of Mike," he broke in, "let's get started on this!" He turned to the cop still struggling with the report. "Where's Peacock? Where's MacNamara? How come the Homicide Squad isn't here yet? Maybe the Commissioner is afraid to disturb his Rover Boys?"

"I don't get you, Lance," mumbled the cop, moistening his pencil.

"Who's on the hunt? What's the report? What have you got on the guy who killed her? He may be half-way to Texas by now! Why don't you—"

"Guy who killed who?" asked the cop.

"This woman!" shouted Lance. "Who murdered her?"

The cop laughed. Dr. Kuppenheimer laughed. The police photographer laughed. Even the janitor laughed.

"What in hell is so funny?" demanded Lance.

A pudgy palm came down in front of his eyes, outstretched, waiting.

"She was taking a bath." Amos Biddle's voice was nice and low. "She slipped on the soap. She fell. She struck her head. She was killed. Five dollars. Please. Thank you."

Lance groaned. He reached for his wallet slowly. A twenty-mule team held it back. He finally brought it out. Eighteen intricate locks bolted it. He got it open.

Amos said, still in the same tone, "The desk told me to get pictures. It's Safety Week. You know? Pictures? Safety?" He pointed to a bill with a stubby finger. "That one. It's a fiver. One bill. Easy to count. Thank you."

He plucked it neatly from the wallet, examined it solemnly on both sides and held it up to the light. Lance eyed him with disgust.

"Three hundred pounds of deceit," he said bitterly.

Amos smirked. You asked for it, Lance told himself; he warned you; you just walked right into it. And now you're walking out.

And then Amos laughed.

Lance stopped. Wait a minute . . . You didn't say you'd get a murder out of this. The bet was to make the story sensational. That's it! He felt more confident. He'd get his money back and five to boot when the *Comet* splashed his story across the front page.

What story? Tenement woman takes bath, slips, falls, cracks head against faucet and dies. So what? Look at that hunk of fat—still laughing. Come on, McCleary, you can make a yarn out of this. It's a cinch. If you can break news, you can make it. Isn't that what Carl always says?

He watched Amos take pictures for the *Comet* Safety Week campaign; pictures of the soap on the floor, the tub, the body.

"What's her name?" he asked.

"Dunno, Lance," said the cop. "Smith when she took this place. Neighbor down the hall knew her as Jones."

Unidentified corpse. Plenty of heart. He'd get punch into this. . . . Cheap joint. Look at the kitchenette. No food. And her shoes—He picked one up. Hm—fancy for a tenement dame. Maybe she was a taxi-dancer? Nah, too old. But how about those Times

Square dolls? Nope, no good. No heart in a taxi-dancer. But a middle-aged one! Show me a guy who'll hire one.

All right, so she went out to a dance. She came in tired and kicked her shoes off. So?

Amos' voice reached him. "How you doing, Lance?"

I'll show him! The thing to do is figure it out logically and change everything. She's alone in the world. Nobody knows where she came from, who she is.

If only she was a movie star! Maybe that's an angle—nope, no good. An heiress—a runaway heiress! *Her?* All right, so she's not an heiress. She's—oh, what the hell!

McCleary, you're slipping. Think, you dope. Now wait, now wait. Let's see . . . She's all alone and—Why alone? She's my cousin. From the West. Came out here to look for me. I can get away with anything because she's my cousin. . . . That stinks. Carl knows I got no relatives.

Dr. Kuppenheimer's raised voice broke into his thoughts.

"*Seventeen* assistant medical examiners and they always send *me* out on these damned accidents! They die from heat exposure, freeze to death, struck by lightning. *I'm* sent out! Baby burned by stove, man falls downstairs, boy shoots self with gun, woman slips in tub. *I'm* sent out! Accidents—accidents—accidents!"

Lance went back to his thoughts. Accident. Come in with an accident buried in adjectives and they'd bury him.

He went into the bathroom. Why? What are you

looking for? There's her washcloth—talc—towel—robe—nightgown. You're stalling, McCleary; you're stuck and you know it and you're stalling. That wasn't you *Time* wrote about. That was a lucky stiff who had a corpse thrown right at him, story, clues—the works. You're a fourflusher. You had a couple lucky breaks and you been coasting on them since.

Lance came out of the bathroom as Dr. Kuppenheimer stalked from the room and the hearse driver and the cop carried the body out after him.

Amos slung the camera across his shoulder and watched Lance with amusement.

"Come on, sucker, you're licked."

Lance swallowed hard.

You going to let him get away with that? Get an angle. Just one lousy little miserable angle. You can blow it up . . . An angle on an accident! You used to cover them. No story then. No story now. Never a story. Just a paragraph hiding behind the ads. McCleary, go back and run copy!

"Stop grinning like an ape!" he snapped at Amos. "I'm thinking."

What a threat. *You're* thinking!

He began one last hopeless round of the room, with the door waiting inevitably. Nothing . . . nothing . . . nothing . . . He passed the dress hanging on the closet door. Her only dress. Poor dame . . . you were almost a story . . .

He joined the waiting Amos, stopped.

"What's the matter?" said the cameraman.

Lance was asking himself the same thing. Why had he stopped? Something . . . He turned and went

back slowly. What was it? The dress?. . . The dress
. . . Oh, yes, the bit of red string stuck to the
shoulder.

McCleary, you're nuts! A piece of red string!

He picked it off—it stuck to the dress. That's
funny. He examined it more closely. Suddenly he felt
that same good old tingling.

McCleary, you're going to ring the bell!

He ran his hand down inside the dress. He found
the safety pin, unfastened it; the red string dropped
into his hand.

He rushed out of the room, past Amos. Then he
halted. Back he went to the goggle-eyed cameraman.

"Give me that five bucks!"

Forty-five minutes later he sauntered up to the city
desk.

"Where've you been?" asked Carl. "They found a
torso of a girl. About nineteen. Attacked and muti-
lated. One Hundred Seventy-second Street and the
Drive . . . We'll blame it on the Gorilla Man. I like
him. He sells papers."

Lance asked, "You know that woman who was
killed in a bathtub last night?"

Carl took a moment to okay the proof on his desk.
"What are you talking about?"

"Carl—look." Lance thumbed through a copy of
the *Comet* to page thirty-three, circled a stick with a
pencil. "That yarn."

Carl glanced at it, returned to the proof. "What
about it?"

"I know who she was."

Seven

Carl kept his eyes down. Oh, God, I knew it, he thought; I knew the moment he walked in and turned to that stick . . .

He continued to play with the proof. He changed a ten-point bold head to eight-point bold caps. Damn that Monroe; fifteen years of story mangling at the slot and still an independent bastard. A boy passed, dropped copy on the desk. Mechanically, Carl killed a cliché in the abortion story; he changed the lead and rememberd an angle to raise it out of the mediocre to page one interest.

And all the time he was frozen, crouching over the desk. He couldn't keep this up indefinitely. Lance was waiting. Soon he must speak—but he was afraid to hear his own voice; it would betray him.

The copy . . . "Prindle." The rewrite man left his typewriter and came up to the desk. "This doctor was in a bank holdup under an alias in August, 1923. Dig out the files and check."

That was good; his judgment and memory were as flawless as ever. Now he could look at Lance. He formed the words carefully. "Who, Lance?"

"She was—"

No, no; not yet. Hold him off. . . . He droned, "Copy boy."

A boy flashed to the desk. "Tell Monroe to go over this stuff with both eyes. Get me cuts and pictures on Charles Eastman."

He handed the boy the copy and heard him say yes, sir, and watched him bring it over to Monroe at the copy desk. *I know who she was.* Why had Lance stopped there? Why hadn't he gone on? Is he feeling me out? *How much does he know?*

He picked up the phone. "Get me Yerkes." He spiked a story with his free hand; his palm was cold with sweat, but the fingers didn't tremble, the hand was steady. "Now what's this all about?" he said to Lance. "I want you to hop on that rape."

He was holding the phone so hard against his ear that the voice at the other end of the line hurt him. It was a laconic, "Yeah, boss."

"Yerkes, McCleary's on that rape. You stick close to the girl's father. Go home with him. I want all the art I can get on her."

He hung up. "Well, Lance? Shoot."

Lance grinned. "This is going to knock you right out of your chair, Carl."

He's *smiling.* . . . What must I say? "Okay, Lance, knock me right out of my chair. Who was she?"

"A Lonely Heart."

Carl waited. But that was it—"A Lonely Heart . . ." Hysteria began to well up in him. He knew if he opened his mouth he would laugh, he would yell with laughter. He dropped his pencil. It rolled and fell to the floor. And when he had picked it up, he was himself again.

"How do you know?" he said.

He watched Lance fumble through his pocket, drop something on the desk. It was a piece of red string, not more than half an inch. Lance looked smugly pleased with himself. It irritated Carl.

"What am I supposed to do," he said, "give you a medal for a puzzle? What is it?"

Lance leaned forward. "It won't be a puzzle to *you* when you recognize it."

What does he mean by that?

Lance tapped the end of the string with his finger. "See that?" The string was fastened to a tiny metal heart, a fragment of red pasteboard still attached to it.

Where did he get it? Did he find it in the room? "What about it?"

Lance pulled out a Lonely Hearts Club card. "Remember this? Look: same string, same little metal heart, same color red cardboard, same—"

"I see it, I see it. But you can't be sure."

Lance held up a small safety pin. "It was pinned to her dress—this was inside—right over her heart."

To her dress? I didn't have time. I had to get out of there. I would have gone crazy. That's why I missed it. "Why didn't you say that in the first place? What's the idea taking such a long time to get to the point?"

Lance spread his hands. "A long time? I'm just telling it to you."

"Well, you've got something." Carl leaned back in his swivel chair and rocked. "When did you see her?"

"About an hour ago."

"What were you doing on a bathtub accident?"

Lance told him briefly. Carl smiled. "Get the five-spot from Biddle?"

"Do you have to ask? Tonight I'll get the other one."

Carl nodded. He had but to say, "Forget it," and the story would be forgotten. What shall I do? But he knew the question was ridiculous. He had no choice. He was an editor. He could have only one impulse, "Print it."

Then he felt it. That familiar warmth that always met an irresistible challenge. Boomerang or beat. It would be his greatest. He would do it.

He looked at Lance fondly. "You're okay." Lance smirked. He never walked away from praise. "You smell a yarn so well you're beginning to smell yourself."

The smirk faded. "Hey, wait a minute!"

"So you found a Lonely Heart. Now isn't that a shortcut to a one-day break."

"What do you want—a serial?"

"You're damn right! And the longer, the better."

Lance took refuge in sarcasm. "What're you going to do—steal her?"

"No, *bury* her."

It took a moment for that to sink in. Then Lance shook his head admiringly. "You son-of-a-gun. . . ."

The publisher of the *Comet*, Frank Madison, who had made a name for himself in the newspaper world as a New Deal hobgoblin when he mixed with both political parties, was an iron-gray, chipmunk-cheeked little ball of fat. He listened to Carl dolefully.

"I want no part of it," he said. "We're running a newspaper, not a funeral parlor."

Carl had expected this. "Listen, Mr. Madison, can't you see the Lonely Hearts reading this story? Can't you hear them say, 'You see, they really look out for us?' They'll tell friends, they'll bring in new members."

Mr. Madison moved his inkwell an inch, put it back again. "But it's so morbid."

Carl kept the impatience out of his voice. "It'll sell papers!"

The publisher rose and walked about the room with short bouncing steps; he adjusted a blind, straightened a picture. "I don't know," he said worriedly, "sometimes, Chapman, you go beyond . . . It's difficult to explain . . . Such a distasteful approach . . ."

"It'll sell papers."

The little man was standing beneath a picture of himself with the Governor. He studied it with pleasure. "Well . . ." He turned a beaming face to his editor.

Light! thought Carl.

"It would be considered a humane gesture on our part, wouldn't it?" said Mr. Madison happily. "Yes! . . . Yes!"

It was as easy as that. But Carl found himself trembling. I'm going to bury her. It came to him shockingly: This is Charlotte! I'm using Charlotte as a springboard for circulation. . . .

The art editor was waiting for him for an okay on the love-nest layout. Johnson of the composing room had a suggestion for the sixty-point head that had given him trouble. A narcotic haul had just been reported by the police. The Sugar King's wire threatened libel unless a retraction was printed to that story. The ferryboat *Robert Fulton* had smashed a barge; and the St. Francis Hospital was ablaze—

Picture!

"Boy!" A copy boy shot to the desk. "Get me all the pictures on the Lonely Hearts Ball."

"Never mind, Carl. I've got it."

It was Lance. He tossed the picture on the desk. "I had a hunch we'd have one on her. Remembered Biddle shooting them in front of their booths. There she is, right in the center."

Carl heard himself say, "You beat me to it."

There she was surrounded by a dozen men and women in front of the Massachusetts booth. Too late to destroy it now. . . .

Lance came around to his side, leaned on the desk to squint at the picture intently. "There's her card. Funny I couldn't find the damn thing anywhere."

She hadn't used her right name. She told him that. Who would recognize this gaunt tubercular woman? Who would remember her as Charlotte?

"Start pounding out that burial," he ordered.

"Old man squawk?"

"At first."

"Save one soul and we double our advertising rates; that turned the trick, huh?"

"There'll be a funeral, too."

"Broadway?"

"Fifth Avenue."

Lance whistled. "The works."

"Paint your picture, Lance. From Potter's Field to Woodlawn Cemetery in one jump."

Lance grinned. "By courtesy of the *Comet*—the paper that buries its dead!"

Eight

"What in hell am I doing here?"

Sometimes Lance puzzled himself. Right now I ought to be at Police Headquarters, he thought. Maybe something's come up. Maybe it's a delivery boy and he's confessing right now. Just my luck they've picked up an escaped lunatic and he's the Gorilla! And I'm here . . . in the Morgue. Maybe it's a butcher. Nah, bet it's one of those strong-arm guys from a circus. I could be fired for not sticking on that story.

But he shrugged and went down the hallway. He had learned not to question his own hunches.

He stopped at an open doorway and said mildly, "Boo."

Small, hazel-eyed Nell Mitchell, who sewed up corpses after the autopsies were completed, looked up from her newspaper.

"McCleary! Darling! Come on in. Long time no see."

He patted her head. "How's Needle Nellie? Heard you're using an electric gadget for that cat-gut."

"You heard right. We're streamlined now. Say, is

this on the level?" She held up the front page of the *Comet*. "Your Lonely Hearts Club really going to bury her?"

"Yep."

Carl had spared no space. Page one was all Lonely Heart. A deep four-column photo layout had the picture of the group surrounding her in front of the booth. A two-column inset was a closeup of the bathtub victim.

Nellie looked at the pictures with renewed interest. "Lance, did they really all wear *hearts* at that shindig?"

"It was just a—Nellie, you're wonderful."

Her eyes widened. "Am I?"

"You just reminded me of something." He went on, over her disappointed *oh*, "Tell me, if you had only one dress and you'd fastened something to it with a safety pin, would you pull the thing off?"

"And make a hole in the dress? You're crazy."

"But if you were burned up about something?"

She reflected. "Even if I had a fight with my boy friend I wouldn't get mad enough to do that."

"Okay. Thanks, Nellie."

"For what?"

He pinched her cheek. "For being wonderful."

She slapped his hand away. "What are you doing around here anyway, when half the noseybodies in New York are looking for the Gorilla?"

"I'm playing hookey."

He went down the corridor.

"Hey, Lance!"

He opened a door and poked his head in. The

woman behind the drawing board peered at him over horn-rimmed glasses. "I could recognize that farmer's walk of yours twenty years from now. Were you going to pass by without dropping in to see me?"

"Hi, Wilma."

She showed an even row of white teeth. He had always liked her teeth. "Nellie told me your paper's burying a Lonely Heart. Whose idea was it—yours or the newsboy's?"

"The newsboy's. What you got?" He looked down over her shoulder. "Hmm—nice colors."

She touched a fine brush to the painting. "Stomach of a poison suicide." She was the Rembrandt of the Morgue. "How's yours?"

He laughed. "How's the family?"

"Fine. Jessie's going on eight and Mickey wants to be Tarzan's son."

"Mickey? He's new, isn't he?"

"Three years new. When are *you* getting married?"

" 'Bye, Wilma," he said firmly.

She shouted after him. "Give my love to Julie!"

In the autopsy room an attendant was washing a slab with a hose. He said, "He's back in his office."

Lance went to Room 218: GENERAL OFFICE of the CHIEF MEDICAL EXAMINER of the CITY OF NEW YORK. He entered without knocking.

Dr. James Francis O'Hanlon popped up from his desk and came forward to shake Lance's hand warmly. He was short, energetic and bald-headed. Now sixty-six, he had been in the M.E.'s office since 1918, performed at least seventy-five hundred autopsies and gained recognition as one of the most erudite medical scientists in the United States.

"Lance McCleary! It's great seeing you again. But you should have been with me yesterday. Three and two on DiMaggio with bases full. Man, what a sock! Right over the shaving ad in right field."

Lance grinned. The doctor hadn't changed. A stubby finger was waved under his nose. "Let me tell you these butter-fingered players today with those lively balls can't hold a candle to the old-timers!"

Selecting a cigar from his desk humidor, Dr. O'Hanlon gestured emphatically with it. "Joe's a good slugger but did he ever bat .400? Cobb did—half-a-dozen times! What would the Tigers have been without Ty Cobb? That thief stole more bases in one season than the whole American League did in a year."

Lance got an inspiration. "How'd you like an Annie Oakley for tomorrow's game?"

The doctor almost swallowed his cigar. "That's the deciding game of the World's Series!"

"Where'd you like to sit?"

"Any seat, any seat!"

"How about behind the screen?"

The Chief Medical Examiner's eyes bulged. "Where I can see the curves break?"

"And watch the old equalizer—"

"—and see how they behave when they have three and two on them!" Dr. O'Hanlon puffed luxuriously. "An Annie Oakley to the last game of the Series . . . Lance, if there's anything I can ever do—"

"You can—now."

"Name it."

"There's somebody here I'd like you to take a look at."

"Friend?"

"Not exactly. She's a story."

"Okay, I'll have Doctor—"

"No, please, I mean you personally."

"Hmm, must be something big. What case?"

"Bathtub accident."

"Yes?"

"She slipped in a tub."

"Yes?"

"Just slipped."

Dr. O'Hanlon gave him a puzzled look. "Who examined her?"

"Dr. Kuppenheimer."

The examiner looked through the papers in the basket on his desk. "Here it is—subarachnoid hemorrhage. Very precise report. What do you want *me* to do?"

"Open her up."

Dr. O'Hanlon chewed the cigar, puffing very slowly as he reread the report. He said, "It's a story you're after, eh? Lance, I want to show you something."

He beckoned. The reporter followed him into the "icebox" where three hundred separate compartments stored sixteen thousand corpses a year. The door of each compartment was numbered.

"If you really want a story," said the examiner, opening door 79, "here's an interesting one for you.

Young Negress, unmarked, apparently peacefully dead—but there's a deep stab wound in her heart that left an almost invisible scratch."

"Nope."

"Hmm. Well, how about this one?" He opened 111. "Show girl. Dead without a bruise; but the autopsy revealed the crushing of the tiny hyoid bone in the throat. She was strangled."

"Nope."

"All right, all right! You want the bathtub girl? You'll get the bathtub girl. What's her name?"

"Unidentified."

"Lance, we've had four this week."

"I can recognize her."

"All right, they're over there." He pointed to the compartments in the corner. "From two-seventy."

Lance opened 270. A fat man on the slab. In 272 was an old woman. In 273 he recognized Lonely Heart.

"Here she is."

The corpse was wheeled into the autopsy room. Dr. O'Hanlon dismissed the attendant.

"Just a waste of time," he said, "but I'll do it for you." He tapped the ash from his cigar, selected a scalpel-sharp butcher knife and began at the head of Lonely Heart.

"You know, Lance, the Baltimore Orioles were the toughest bunch of players that ever got together." He sawed off the top of the skull and examined the brain. "Each one of 'em loved to scrap. That was when Johnnie McGraw played outfield for them."

He was about to make an incision at the base of the throat to cut straight down through the abdomen when Lance found his tongue.

"Uh—uh—Doctor—"

Cigar jutting from the corner of his mouth, the examiner looked up. "Yes?"

"The *Comet's* burying her."

"Indeed? Why?"

"She was a member of the *Comet* Lonely Hearts Club."

"I see . . . Evening gown I suppose. You want all marks concealed." He made an incision at the lower end of the breastbone. "Ball players they call 'em today! Why, back in fourteen when the Braves battled the Athletics—that was the day of real ball players. You young fellows today miss plenty. That million dollar infield they had! Stuffy McInnes on first"—he branched the cut to extend to the armpits— "Jack Barry as shortstop, Eddie Collins on second and Home-Run Baker on third."

Lance had seen many autopsies. But they always got him. He fought against being sick over the corpse. Dimly through the roaring in his ears he heard, "In the good old days they used to warm up two, even three pitchers before a game. If a twirler didn't have the stuff, another boy'd be sent in to pitch. A catcher can always tell if a pitcher's ready. But today—bah!"

The cut was completed.

"Hurlers they call 'em today. That's a laugh. Why Walsh's spitball and Christy's fadeaway—*they* were something! Christy Mathewson—what a man!"

Dr. O'Hanlon put the cigar down, gently compressed her lungs and stomach and sniffed at her lips. Lance quickly averted his head. He knew the examiner was sniffing for the odor of bitter almonds, evidence of cyanide of potassium or hydrocyanic acid.

Dr. O'Hanlon straightened, relit his cigar. No odor. He puffed with enjoyment as he opened the thoracic cage, removed the heart, weighed it. He cut the chambers open and looked at them, examining the coronary arteries.

"And what about Big Train Johnson who smoked them over the plate for twenty-one delirious summers? Where can you see 'em pitch like that today? And Three-Fingered Brown's hook and Carl Mays' submarine and Grover Cleveland Alexander."

He cut out the lungs, weighed them, then pressed them with his fingers as if they were a blown-up balloon.

"She didn't drown in the bathtub, Lance. Lungs aren't water-logged. This corpse was a corpse before it struck the water."

"Her head struck the faucet in the tub," explained Lance.

"That's what killed her. See those bruises on the body? She must have hit every part of the tub."

Lance was perspiring. Dr. O'Hanlon was removing the stomach.

"About the only lad left today who can throw a real screwball is Carl Hubbell . . . The sinkers they throw these days are nothing but old-fashioned drops!"

He groped inside the cadaver, shook his head, mumbled, "Lost . . ."

Lance leaned forward, waiting tensely. Was something wrong? Had Dr. O'Hanlon discovered a flaw? A lead? What was it?

"Lost," repeated the examiner. "It's a lost art today—stealing bases."

Lance stepped back, tried to take a deep breath, found he couldn't. The room. It felt stuffy. He knew it wasn't. Ventilation was excellent. But the doctor's deft hands . . .

He cut out the intestines carefully, went over them foot by foot.

He examined her organs for any evidence of criminal attack or operation. "You understand I'm not crabbing, Lance. Lots of good talent around these days. But nothing great. Nothing like Chief Bender the Indian and Eddie Plank and Rogers Hornsby."

Lance stared straight ahead, keeping his eyes from the red opening below, waiting, hoping, knowing this was, as he had been forewarned, a waste of time.

"Tomorrow when I watch 'em cross the dish and powder homers," said the examiner, taking the kidneys out, "I'll be thinking of Frankie."

It took a full moment for Lance to piece the sentence together. "Frankie?"

Dr. O'Hanlon dropped the kidneys on the slab and turned the corpse over. "He's that young fellow working in the back room, the museum, collecting hearts. He usually goes with me."

He cut through the vertebrae and exposed the spinal canal. Lance lowered his eyes for a split-second. The canal was filled with blood.

Dr. O'Hanlon looked up, his eyes twinkling hopefully. "Say, Lance, you don't think you could—uh—fix up another ducat for Frankie, do you? Hmm?"

Lance staring at the wall could still see the red canal. "Sure, sure," he said.

"That's great!" The examiner turned the corpse over on its back again. "Only this morning I was telling Frankie about the game in twenty-five when I first heard a slugger squawk to the ump—'You can't hit 'em when you can't see 'em!'"

He chuckled at the memory of that moment and gently proceeded to replace the vital organs.

"First in war, first in peace and last in the American League—the Washington Senators!" he announced dramatically, burst into laughter and as he replaced the heart, shook his head reminiscently. "Yes, sir, Lance, them were the days . . ."

It was over. Lance had wasted the examiner's time and his own. His hunch was wrong and he needed a drink.

"Dr. Kuppenheimer's diagnosis was right, Lance. Blood clot's there from the faucet blow. Her spinal canal filled with blood is evidence of intracranial hemorrhage. That's all there is to it. This corpse isn't worth a line except as a warning to be more cautious getting in and out of bathtubs."

"You're *sure* there's nothing else?"

The examiner looked at him queerly, then smiled. "What's the matter with you, Lance? You used to be able to recognize a story at a glance. I'll get Nellie to sew this up now. Any kind of evening dress will do. No scars will show."

Lance knew he was going down for the last time.

He tried once more. "Will you do me one last favor?"

"Now what?"

"Will you scrape her?"

"Lance," Dr. O'Hanlon shook his head impatiently, "you ought to be ashamed of yourself. But an Annie Oakley's an Annie Oakley! You want her scraped? She'll be scraped."

He lifted the hands of the corpse and with a toothpick cleaned out what he found under the nails of the right hand, transferred it to a slide and slipped it under the microscope. Then he gave a soft whistle of surprise.

Lance jumped. "What is it?"

The examiner scratched his chin. He wasn't thinking baseball now. Something was up! He stared at Lance incredulously. "How do you do it?"

Lance's voice cracked. "How do I do what?"

"Take a look for yourself."

Lance bent over the microscope. Suddenly he felt that same good old tingling.

"It looks like—it looks like—"

"It is. Those are scraps of flesh and bits of hair."

Nine

He knows . . .

Carl closed his eyes. The flowers . . . once he had gone through a perfume factory and the steam had become a stink that made him retch. I won't be sick . . .

They had been talking about pink. Somewhere an organ was playing.

"Because she was murdered."

He tried to turn but his body was weighted, leaden. He saw the rococo entrance and the maroon rug and the six statues standing at attention. They were all the same height, they all wore cutaways. They looked alike. One of them moved.

"Yes, this is Lloyd's Funeral Parlor. This way. Yes, madam, this is Lloyd's Funeral Parlor. This way."

"There is no color or design unlisted in our catalogue, Mr. Chapman."

"If we knew what her favorite color was, Mr. Chapman."

Who else knows?

"You're not going to bury her tomorrow. She was murdered."

He saw Lance's face, dead-pan. "It's exclusive."

"If we knew what her favorite color was, Mr. Chapman."

She wore pink on their honeymoon . . . Revere Beach . . . New York and Jane Cowl in *Smilin' Through*. She wore pink . . .

"Make it pink."

"Not pink!"

Julie was wearing a pink sweater so Lance didn't want pink. She was pretty and young and fresh so Lance didn't want pink.

Carl saw eight caskets, each opened, each mounted on a pedestal, each bathed in indirect lighting.

"We're picking out a nice one for Lonely Heart, Lance. What are *you*—"

"The desk told me you were here."

"So?"

"So I shot over as soon as I could."

"What for? To tell me you don't like pink?"

Julie had been thrilled. "Can I go with you, Mr. Chapman? I want to help . . ."

Lance didn't like it. "What did you bring *her* here for?"

"We're picking out a nice one for Lonely Heart, Lance. What are *you*—"

Lloyd's had the best. It looked like the Roxy. Lloyd was an oily, smug merchant of death.

"Life ebbs, fails, hangs by a thread . . . Death is beautiful . . ."

There were sounds like a muffled drum from another room . . . somewhere a choir was singing.

"Lance, one of these days I'm going to break your

neck. Where the hell've you been the last four hours?
I told you the Gorilla—"

"The Morgue. I've been visiting Lonely Heart."

"Forget her. She's only good for the funeral. I
told you to forget her."

Lloyd coughed. He was nervous. Too much disturbance. This is a mortuary, gentlemen. Please,
please, please . . .

"You're not going to bury her tomorrow, Carl."

"Why not?"

"Because she was murdered."

"Julie, take care of it. Pink. Blue. Yellow. Any
color. Pick out a color. Come on, Lance."

There were candles in the corridors. There were
candles in all the corridors.

"Why didn't you call?"

"Not the Gorilla, Carl."

"Quit stalling!"

Gentlemen, please . . . please . . .

"Tell anyone at the paper?"

"Nope. It's our baby—yours and mine."

"Who opened her up?"

"O'Hanlon."

O'Hanlon. That meant the rounds. Cops, detectives, manhunts. The whole city would be up in arms.

How did he find out? What did I forget? Where
did I slip?

"Scraps of flesh and bits of hair under her finger-
nails. I saw them."

Carl saw her reach out, clawing. He felt her nails
rake his cheek again.

"Scraps of flesh and bits of hair under her finger-nails. A man's. They know because of the hair."

They know, they know, they know . . .

"When are you going to bury her, Carl?"

"What fool question is that? You ought to know, you wrote the hearts and flowers."

Flowers were for the sick, flowers were for the dead.

"What was the cause of death?"

"Cracked skull."

He saw his handkerchief wiping the blood from his fingers, one by one.

"How was she killed?"

You know. You say you know. Then how was she killed? How was she killed?

"He knocked her down. There was a bed. Iron." Lance held out one hand. "Head." He held out the other. "Foot of bed." He brought his hands together. He made a noise with his mouth. "Song-and-dance for page one."

He saw her on the floor, motionless . . . The foot of the bed . . . She's dead but I'm alive. I can move. He went into the corridor with Lance.

"We're picking out a nice one for Lonely Heart, Lance."

"The cops went over everything in the room. They found blood on the foot of the bed."

He'd washed it off. He threw the handkerchief down the sewer. There was no blood. He'd washed it off . . .

"The guy thought he washed it off."

"How do they know it's a man?"

"The hair . . . O'Hanlon proved she was dead in the bedroom."

When he was a little boy he was safe in his bedroom.

"Lance, what made you—"

"One of my hunches . . . The way *I* figure it . . ." The way *I* figure it, the way *I* figure it . . .

"She picked up a boy friend at the Ball and took him home with her to her room. Then when everything was set for the business they had a battle. He socked her. He knocked her down and she hit her head against the foot of the bed. When he saw that he'd killed her, he got panicky and tried to make it look like an accident."

That was the way Lance figured it. He was smart.

"One of my hunches."

He saw Lance strutting. You're smart, Lance, and I must be careful. Careful. Careful.

You can't bury her tomorrow. Because she was murdered.

That wasn't careful.

"You mean he dragged her to the tub?"

"Sure. Turned the tap on and held her up so her head would smash on the faucet."

Would? It had. He'd measured carefully . . .

"Then he set the stage—didn't leave out an effect. Must be a pretty smart guy at that. Didn't miss a trick."

That's what they called Julie—a cute trick. She was in love with Lance. She showed it and didn't care. She wanted to marry Lance. She said she'd wait, but she'd wear a wedding ring—

"Hey, wait a minute—there was a mark on her finger, third, left hand."

"There was one thing I wouldn't pawn!"

"He removed everything. Even ripped off her club card, but he left a piece of red string for Hawk-eye to find."

That was a mistake. Oh, that was a mistake. But that wasn't the only mistake. He shouldn't have killed her that way. He should have held her under the water in the tub. Then there would have been no marks . . .

"And the accident would have worked."

Would have? It will still work. It will! It will!

Ten

All day Lonely Heart lay in state in the domed rotunda of Lloyd's Funeral Parlor. A shaft of sun angled down to her through tall windows, bright, solid, like a pillar of light.

All day a mob filed past her slowly in a carefully controlled line, while newsreels cranked and Amos Biddle was camera-happy. Tears were contagious.

Everything had been arranged, everything timed. No detail had been overlooked even to encouraged weeping and purchased hysteria. New York loved a show. Carl was giving it one.

ADIEU, LONELY HEART—that had been his bannerline. And he had set her obituary in the center of page one in ten and twelve point, two columns part copy, part nightmare, and boxed with a heavy black border. Eight point wasn't big enough. Big type always moved *Comet* readers.

"Tomorrow New York will be a city of whispers.

"Tomorrow New York will mourn.

"Tomorrow fourteen thousand members of the *Comet* Lonely Hearts Club will grieve.

"Tomorrow Lonely Heart will be buried.

"To the members of the Club this newspaper bows in tribute. To them, the *Comet* says: 'Lonely Heart was one of your own. She was one of you.'

"Sleep, Lonely Heart . . . Sleep the everlasting sleep . . . Sleep peacefully . . . for unknown, you are not unclaimed, you are not unwanted, you are not unremembered."

Sure it was cheap, sure it was sensationalism. But why try to emerge from the red light district of journalism when horseplay like lowering the flag of the *Comet* to half-mast rang the bell and every sob was a sale?

The procession came off like clockwork . . . a police band . . . a police escort . . . crowds in the streets . . . At the cemetery a host of small boys clung to the trees. That was good for a three-column photo.

He recalled the argument he had had with his publisher. Madison had balked: an ordinary grave was good enough for anyone else; why the expense of a private crypt for her? But Carl had known how to handle him. An ordinary grave would give the *Comet* publicity, but the ivy-covered, peak-roofed mausoleum spelled prestige. All he had to do then was show Madison a picture of it. Madison loved pictures.

Then as the choir on the hillside sang "Lead, Kindly Light," six officers of the Lonely Hearts Club carried their burden into the flower-softened interior of the tomb.

For the first time he forced himself to look at the casket he had chosen.

Now . . .

But he felt nothing. Lonely Heart was being buried. She was not Charlotte. She was not guilt and punishment. She was no longer *anything*. She was just a story. He had won . . .

What a wonderful morning!

And a woman standing beside him turned to him with handkerchief pressed to her lips and sobbed, "It's the most wonderful funeral I ever saw. Who's dead?"

Julie sighed.

"Oh, Mr. Chapman, it was a beautiful funeral."

Carl scribbled figures in the upper corner of a sheet of copy and with an expert twist sent it sailing onto the big horseshoe desk near his own. Sweet Julie. She had wept at the funeral in all sincerity.

He looked up at her. "Yes, Julie, it was beautiful."

Lance walked up to the desk. "What?"

"The funeral," said Julie.

Lance grunted. He dropped his copy on the desk. "If I have to write any more of this stuff, I'll need a handkerchief for my typewriter."

It amused Carl: Mutt and Jeff—Lance and Julie. He had been so busy he had almost forgotten the legendary romance of the city room. Everyone on the staff had given up laying bets on the day when Lance would give in. One day he would get tired . . .

"When you two kids are ready to buy that ring—" said Carl.

Lance coughed loudly. "What was that new angle you wanted to tell me about?"

"Don't interrupt," said Julie.

"Go type something, honey," advised Lance.

"This Lonely Heart business must be getting under your skin," he told Carl balefully. "Next thing you know, you'll be running a marriage bureau."

Carl couldn't resist. "Not a bad idea. With a little art, it'll make a nice feature for the Saturday supplement."

That held Lance. Then Carl relented. "All right, Julie; about that church bazaar next week, you can start right on it. We'll give it the build-up you want."

Lance waited until she had left. "Now that Cupid's through shooting arrows into a guy's back, can we be boys together again? What you got?"

"A subsidiary to the Lonely Hearts Club."

"We're off again! *Nu?*"

"Detectives."

"No kidding!"

"Yep. The Lonely Heart Detectives."

Lance leaned against the desk as if he were exhausted, got right up again and moved the spike away from him. "Milked to the last drop."

Carl loved him. You red-headed Irishman. I never have to explain to you. And no matter what wild stunt I throw into your lap, you always come through. If only you knew what a good mood I'm in, you'd tap me for a raise—and I'd give it to you. If only you knew . . .

"I'm only beginning," he said.

"What do you want the Charlie Chans of the *Comet* to do?"

"Avenge Lonely Heart."

Lance yawned. "You're breaking mine."

"We'll have every member of the club loose on the city. They'll search cellars—"

"Patrol roofs," droned Lance.

"—scour the parks—"

"Don't forget the ventilating systems!"

"Right. We'll make it a personal issue."

Lance scratched his ear. "I knew that was coming."

"It'll be the personal duty of every member to help the police find the man who killed her."

"Bingo!"

"Nobody but a subscriber gets a badge."

"Naturally." Lance started away.

"Stand by, baby," said Carl, "you're going to take a bow."

He turned to his staff. "Boys, we've given birth to a murder. Lance, here, is the papa."

Lance took the bow.

"Now this is no ordinary baby," Carl went on, pushing back his chair and rising. "We're going to feed it and watch it and make it grow. But it's *our* baby—remember that. As long as we hang on to it, we sell papers. We don't want any other sheet to move in on it—no godfathers."

He seldom made a speech. They were listening attentively.

"Some of you ambitious Sherlocks might stumble on a clue. Next thing, the law follows through and nabs the killer. Then what? He's only good for a hearing, a trial and an execution. Our baby is good forever. Forget the law. If any of you get a smell of a lead on the killer—bring it to me."

It was funny, and only he could laugh . . .

BOOK TWO

Eleven

The shop was in the middle of the block in a two-story, puce-colored building, its doors wide open, three huge globes clustered together in rust over the entrance. On one side gutter vaudeville, on the other a mucky cafeteria.

Carl dismissed his cab three blocks down. He stood on Grand and Bowery. All about lay the Bowery. It was a long time since his rewrite days when all this had been familiar ground, longer still since that first day when he had stood, a newcomer to New York, at this intersection. The smell was the same.

Still the same junk wagons drawn by skinny horses . . . shiny pretzels on sticks . . . wax flowers . . . peanut stands . . . second-hand clothes, molded and dusty . . . shoes on strings over doorways . . . overalls displayed on counters but prudently fastened to them . . . hot dogs . . . soup 5¢ . . . malteds 7¢ . . . shaves 10¢ . . . Still saloons, flophouses, cheap theaters, restaurants, labor agencies, missions . . .

But it had changed, even since those latter *Chronicle* days the Bowery had changed. Only the bums endured . . . the same bums . . .

A sight-seeing bus discharged twittering tourists awed at seeing the Bowery as if it were still the roué, fascinated by the bored spiel of the guide. Carl walked on slowly, oblivious to them. He felt again the thrill of that first day. *"This is the Bowery!"* He felt again the nostalgia for a past he had never known.

He had an odd sense that past and present were fused, so that he could not differentiate between what he himself had seen and known and what he had read and heard . . .

The Five Points Mission to which, after his great anti-slavery speech at Cooper Union, Lincoln had strolled to investigate the poor in the lusty, impudent, vile vagabondry of that day . . . The Red Roach, one-time famous house of prostitution, now a bird and animal store: "Our Agents Are Busy in Far-off Africa, South America and India" . . . The Tub of Blood, now a flophouse . . . McGurk's Suicide Hall, now a rescue mission . . .

Once a portrait of Sophie the Scrubwoman had hung in the Rescue Mission. Sophie was gone and a lumber dealer whose stock was all under roof was there instead . . . A.C.B.'s jewelry store where Captain Cornelius Vanderbilt bought a "diamond" pin for $1.25, and to which Diamond Jim Brady brought his fat jewel-studded watch for repairs once a week. It was a hotel-equipment store now.

There was Dickson's! One window was yesterday, still brazenly displaying likenesses of President Cleveland, John Drew and General Grant as specimens of the "Artistic Work Done Within"; the other was today—it featured photographs for passports, sweethearts, cab drivers' licenses . . .

Across from it should be the Doyer Dump where he had gambled his earnings from the *Chronicle*. You went through the brown door and up two flights . . . The brown door was two doors and they were red and the place was a drygoods jobber's now.

Hamburgers one could reach out and touch sizzled invitingly. The stove had been moved to the right and a new sign read: "Beef stew with bread and coffee with cream 10¢" It used to be 4¢. He had never had enough to eat in those days. He was almost tempted to buy and eat a hamburger for the hunger he had known then. But his stomach rebelled.

There was the same old window-card in a store:

**LOOK HOW
CHEAP
THE GOODS**

A hand-lettered poster on the front of a building was new:

**DO YOU WANT A NEW THRILL?
LET JESUS
DYNAMITE
SIN OUT OF YOUR SOUL**

Jesus Saves . . . Confess Your Sins . . . Beds 15¢ Beds . . . Men's pants: $1.49 . . . Jewelry stores, dozens of them, featuring cheap flashy ornaments . . . Overhead the roaring elevated . . . pitchmen bark-

ing . . . watches, razor blades . . . knives . . . car
polish, shoe polish, grease remover, dirt remover . . .

Where once had been the Occidental Hotel, Chuck
Connors, Sloppy Mag McUnsky, Frisco Nell, the *old*
Olliffe Pharmacy. And Gold-Tooth Fannie, that ami-
able lady of the night who gave away food from a
torchlit cart on cold winter dawns to the outcasts . . .

Had he actually seen Mr. Zero feeding the hungry
in his Tub? Had they been real—the street stabbings,
that sailor robbed and beaten to death by a gang of
hoodlums, the busking act that degenerated into a
fatal tussle with "inside" entertainers, sending three
dancers to Potter's Field and six singers to Bellevue?

It seemed so long ago, so far away . . .

But he was approaching the shop. He had not had
time to get down until today.

What could she have pawned?

He fingered the ticket in his pocket. He didn't have
to look at it. He could sit down right now and set it
up word for word, character for character, in the
right caps and the same rules. He knew what was in
italics and what was boldface.

"Socks, mister? Imported. T'ree pairs f' twenny-
seven cents."

He would get it over with quickly. He would walk
in, hand the ticket across the counter to a clerk, ask
"How much?" pay him and walk out again.

What could she have pawned?

What if he were asked, "What did you pawn?" It
saved time for the clerks. What did you pawn—a
camera? And to the camera-shelf. A coat? To the

clothes-rack. A suitcase? To the baggage room. Jewelry? To the safe.

What could he say? If he hesitated . . .

She may have told them not to honor the ticket to anyone but herself. Or wasn't that a law? There had been a story . . . last June. He remembered giving it a head. An A.P. story. Oh, yes, a new law about pawn shops—only owners could get their stuff. But that was a midwest yarn. Not here.

What could she have pawned?

A picture? A locket? I gave her a locket once for her birthday. Couldn't afford much, paid only fifteen dollars for it. Maybe she got two dollars on it—if she was lucky. Didn't I give her a watch? To Charlotte from John with love. No, that was the ring . . .

"Shine, mister?"

Do they list in their books whether it's a man or a woman who has pawned something? I could check . . . I could say it was my sister or a friend . . .

This is senseless! I'm taking the whole thing too seriously. I ought to tear the ticket up and forget it. She couldn't have pawned anything important—she didn't have anything. I'll feel like a fool if—

"Pardon me, sir, can you tell me where the Park Place subway station is?"

It was an elderly woman with a rosy face and a funny black hat.

He smiled at her. "Go to the other side of the park —" He looked beyond her. They were on the other side of the park. He had walked across and up Broadway without realizing it. He was on Chambers now.

He changed the direction of his pointing finger. "Right there—near the Woolworth Building."

He crossed the park again quickly, angry with himself, and went back to the shop.

Through the fly-specked window a dumpy man with a patch of black fuzz on the top of his head looked up over his glasses from behind the counter. Carl averted his eyes.

What am I waiting for? Just walk in—

"*Mister* Chapman!"

Even before the hand came down on his shoulder and the whisky cough exploded behind him, he knew who it was. Pop Farnsworth. Of all the times to be held up by this panhandling rummy! Carl turned impatiently.

"Hello, Pop."

The grubby old man with loose bloated cheeks and watered eyes, bowed. His dirty collar was a fixture held together by an old safety pin. His hat was a bet Carl had lost to him on the Sacco-Vanzetti trial. He rubbed a sleeve across his red leaking nose and laughed.

"Well—Carl Chapman, away from his desk!"

He laughed again. Carl took a step away. At any point Pop's insane sense of humor might explode in an hysteria that would attract a crowd. But Pop's hand fastened on his arm.

"Doing business down here? Leave it to me. Know him—good friend of mine." Pop winked. "Get you a good price."

"Never mind." Carl jerked free.

"Ah, now, Carl, don't be like that. It's me—Pop."

Me—Pop . . . Once this sodden, noisy, unshaven wreck had been the top-flight journalist on Park Row. It was hard to believe. Carl had genuine respect for the newspaperman Pop had been; he felt only disgust for what Pop was now.

"Here." He pulled out a quarter, thrust it at the old man and walked off.

His fingers had touched the ticket. He would get rid of it as soon as he had lost Pop. He was sick of the whole business.

He heard Pop's shuffle behind him. Carl increased his pace. "Don't bother me!"

But Pop was keeping up with him. "How about a half-a-buck?" He was sure of himself, buoyant, undisturbed.

"Beat it!"

"But, Carl—two-bits! It's not even a pick-me-up."

A round-shouldered son of Shem leaning against his second-hand clothes store front, chuckled. A fat tramp passing, called out, "Work him over right, Pop!"

Carl was losing his temper. "Quit pestering me!"

Pop clucked. "For shame—Carl Chapman—two-bits!"

"Pop—I'm busy!"

"Ah, yes . . . too busy for an old friend . . ." Speech was undeterred by speed. Pop could go on, block after block . . .

Carl stopped. "All right, all right!" He jammed his hand into his pocket, pulled out a wadded bill and stuffed it into Pop's hand. "Don't bother me for a year!"

He didn't wait. They were near the corner. He rounded it briskly. Now he would have to circle the block . . .

"Hey, Carl!"

Pop was still following him. Now what! Carl ducked into the nearest hallway. On either side of him were large garish drawings—a ship in full sail, a cross with a flaming heart in its center, St. George and the dragon, a pig's head, ships' propellers, nudes with upstanding breasts, Peter and the crowing cock. It was the entrance to a tattooing establishment. Damn that drunk!

"Carl! Mr. Chapman!"

He slid behind a six-foot sign: Rock of Ages—$1.50. Pop went by, wheezing, grunting.

Carl stayed in his refuge for hot uncounted minutes. When he emerged, cautiously, Pop had gone.

Enough time wasted. There was work waiting for him. That convention story. The Governor of Maine was coming in. Copy was piling up on his desk. The meeting with the *Comet's* lawyers on the defamation of character suit. He hurried toward the shop.

He was impatient to have it over with. He reached for the ticket. His groping fingers missed it. He stopped and searched his pocket carefully. The ticket was gone. He had lost it.

Perhaps when he had given Pop that quarter . . . He had been standing—there . . . Perhaps, absent-mindedly, he had put it in another pocket . . . He went through them all while he scanned the sidewalk.

"Lose somethin', mister?"

He looked up. A circle of faces, interested, derelict. He walked away from them retracing his steps, his eyes searching . . . He had gone this way . . . he had stopped here to give Pop the bill . . . turned the corner . . . The Rock of Ages. Perhaps it had dropped from his pocket . . .

He went behind it, crouched. Dirt, tinfoil, used matches, pornographic postcard, bottle caps, cigarette butts.

"If you're really religious, mister, I can put the Rock on for fifty dollars. Cover the whole back. Three colors."

He straightened. An anemic man in a smock with a Vandyke beard and crooked pince-nez beckoned.

"I'm Professor Hall. Come right in. Navy man?"

Carl held up a finger to a cruising cab. His temples throbbed with exasperation at the thought of the time thrown to the winds . . . his own fears . . .

But as the cab started, he shrugged. Well, the ticket was lost. So that was that. He could forget it.

Twelve

Pop shuffled down Chatham Square. He crossed in front of the Newsboys' Home, passed Hearst's old Journal building on the corner and rolled into a small saloon across from the defunct circulation platform.

He spread himself at the bar and brought his fist down on it.

"Ten whiskies!"

The only bartender in the place, a man as old as Pop, with a raw complexion and a face that was empty of everything, moved slowly toward him behind the bar, wiping a glass with a dirty towel. He weighed three hundred and seven pounds; a photograph of him above the register proclaimed this to the ounce, with a caption: "The Fattest Bartender in New York."

"Line 'em up, Charlie—right here." Pop drew a line across the dank bar.

"Now, Mr. Farnsworth," said Charlie respectfully, "you know the boss told me—"

Pop waved the bill Carl had given him, let it drop to the bar. Charlie picked it up, examined it closely.

"I didn't make it, my boy," said Pop dryly.

Charlie hesitated. "Don't you want to hold out fifteen cents for a flop?"

Pop shook his head in a beatific negative. Charlie sighed. "Ten it is."

He lined them up and watched the spendthrift down three without a stop.

"Awful stuff," said Pop.

"Yeah." Charlie leaned a melancholy elbow on the bar. "Remember the first time I served you?"

Pop picked up the fourth drink. "Let me see . . . Afternoon . . . October . . . That's it, October eighteenth, 1910. I just got back from the bombing of the Los Angeles *Times*."

Charlie beamed. "And you came right to Lüchow's. My first day there."

Pop gestured with the drink. "Lüchow's."

"That beer . . ." said Charlie dreamily.

"Beer? Liquid gold!" Pop closed his eyes and swayed. "Tiny raw onions with every seidel . . . pretzels and cheese and sausage and pickles and meats —free—with every dripping schooner . . ."

He eyed the fifth drink with disgust. But drank it.

Charlie scratched his stomach. "Ain't what it used to be, Lüchow's . . ." He smiled in fond memory. "Remember the night Caruso sang for us?"

Pop set an empty glass in front of the mellow Charlie. "The bar," pushed another opposite it, "The pastry-counter," and made a cross in front of the second glass. "There he was . . . Do I remember?"

Charlie stared at the mark with pleasure. "He ate up every bit of cheese cake. . . . Him and that

Victor Herbert, they both had a record of twenty-two seidel of Würzburger—without getting up!"

"*My* record was thirty," said Pop nonchalantly. He made the sixth drink disappear, cleared his throat and began to sing.

"Just order two seid-els of lager, or three,
If I don't want to drink it, please force it on me,
The Rhine may be fine but a cold stein for mi-ine—"

Charlie joined him: " 'Down where the Würz-burger flows . . .' "

They laughed. Charlie blew his nose. "Ah, that Nora Bayes . . ."

" 'What good is water when you're dry?' " chanted Pop.

Charlie sang, " 'For a ship to sail on it is fine; but to drink—well not me.' She sung it different," he said modestly.

Pop, strangling over the sixth drink, wheezed, "Don't stop, my boy, don't stop. Give us that little ditty you—"

"Oh, no, Mr. Farnsworth, I couldn't."

"Now, now, Charlie. Right after poor Louis Zucker rendered the classics on the piano, you came out . . ."

Charlie set both hands on the bar, fixed his eyes on the opposite wall and put his heart into the song:

"Oh where, oh where iss mein little dog gone?
Oh where, oh where can he be?
Mit his ears cut shord und his tail cut long—
Oh where, oh where can he be?"

Pop applauded vigorously. "Wonderful! Wonderful!" Charlie blushed. Pop downed his seventh drink. "Hope I can stand it to the tenth."

He gulped the last three in rapid succession, clung to the bar and shuddered violently. Then he recovered.

"Ah, me . . . Charlie, I am a new man. 'Richard is himself again.' "

"Yes, Mr. Farnsworth."

Pop pushed himself away from the bar, achieved an equilibrium. Charlie leaned over the bar as far as his paunch would allow.

"Mr. Farnsworth, I can let you have that fifteen cents for a flop," he whispered.

On his way out, Pop waved a graceful hand. "My boy, I am grateful. But"—he pointed to the bill Charlie had not rung up—"there are more like that, many more. I shall return with them anon . . . 'Boot, saddle, to horse, and away.' "

Veering and tacking, sonorously greeting alike those he knew and those he didn't, he made his way to the *Comet* building . . .

He peered cautiously from behind the row of lockers dividing the editorial department from the business offices. Carl wasn't at his desk. He moved quickly to the dead-end section of the floor. Julie Allison's cave was there.

She was almost hidden behind the pamphlets, mimeographed announcements, religious books, publicity puffs and stacks of invitations to Bible classes, Sunday schools, bazaars and Saturday night raffles piled on her ancient roll-top desk. The walls were covered with framed quotations from the Holy Book, full page cutouts of her department, autographed photos of priests, ministers, rabbis and Father Divine.

He took off his hat and waited, humble, silent. But she didn't see him. It spoiled his effect. He had to cough.

"Hello, Mr. Farnsworth. Come in." She removed a batch of papers from a worn leather chair. "Sit down."

"No . . . I am not worthy."

Julie's eyes twinkled. "What have you been up to now?"

Pop came in and sat gingerly on the edge of the chair. "I was compelled to choose between right and wrong, between common sense and heroic sacrifice."

"My goodness."

"It was a problem never to be solved by the logarithms of philosophy, but by the simple arithmetic of the heart—and the lack of rupees."

"Oh, you mean you need money."

He blinked rapidly, gulped and blew his nose. Then as that didn't seem to move her, he added a touch of his grimy handkerchief to his eyes.

Julie patted his knee. "Please don't cry, Mr. Farnsworth. You know I'll help you."

"You have already done more for me than any other mortal." Pop groaned. "Oh, Miss Allison—I can never find myself again until I have righted a great wrong."

She hitched herself forward in the big swivel chair

that could have held two of her. "Tell me, Mr. Farnsworth; it will make you feel better."

"I have committed sacrilege."

She looked startled. "Against what?"

He fumbled through his pocket and brought out a green pasteboard. His hands were shaking involuntarily; he eyed them with artistic approval.

"Here," he said; "it represents a treasure I had kept for years."

"Why, it's a pawn ticket."

He breathed heavily. "Aye . . ."

"Mr. Farnsworth—" she leveled a finger at him, "what did you pawn?"

It was time for a sob. He sobbed. "My poor mother's picture."

She looked thoughtful and puzzled, so he went on at once. "You hate me. You despise me. You loathe this shameless sinner before you, this despicable unfortunate who has an inferno raging in his heart, this Rabelaisian vulgarian whose earthiness—"

"How much do you need?"

"Ten dollars."

"Ten dollars—for a picture?"

"Framed in gold," said Pop hastily. "But it is the picture I want. The rest is tinsel. You may have it. Gold, silver, bronze—all meaningless to me."

Julie rummaged in her purse; she looked troubled. "Ten dollars is a lot of money . . . I don't think I have—no, I haven't. We'll have to ask Mr. McCleary to help us."

"No!" Pop was on his feet.

"But why not?"

"He—uh—won't understand."

"Mr. Farnsworth, you're mistaken." Julie was in earnest. "Mr. McCleary is the kindest—"

"Some other time, Miss Allison." Pop was firm. "Good-by."

He picked up the ticket, turned and came face to face with Lance lounging in the doorway. Lance grinned.

"How much you tapping her for this time?"

Julie's eyes brightened with the pleased smile they always had when she saw him. "You're just in time. Mr. Farnsworth has a problem."

"She's nice," he told Pop. "She means you're thirsty."

Pop placed a paternal hand on Lance's shoulder. "Lance, my lad, you are my bosom friend. I am devoted to you. You are youth. You belong to an adventurous tribe of males—undaunted—colors flying . . ."

Lance tipped a wink to Julie, but she was watching the old man, listening to every word.

Pop sighed gustily. Lance turned his face away. "Ah, were I but young again! 'Aye, a chiel's amang ye takin' notes and faith, he'll prent it.' " He stepped backward, measured Lance dramatically. " 'Some tell, some bear, some judge of news' "—it was an accolade to Lance—"some make it!"

"He means you!" cried Julie. "Isn't that beautiful?"

Lance laughed. "All right, Pop; what's bothering you?"

"My conscience."

"Come again?"

Pop frowned righteously. "I am resolute in my sincerity." He showed Lance the ticket, dug up another sigh. "My abnegation . . ."

Lance squinted at it. "Where'd you steal it?"

"Steal it? Shades of Barabbas, you think me a rapparee? It is mine! I had to sacrifice honor for it."

"Whose?"

Pop glared. "I was forced to impignorate my mother's portrait for a few pieces of gold."

"Ve-ry good," drawled Lance judiciously. "Anyway, it's different."

Julie pulled at his sleeve. "Don't, Mr. McCleary. Can't you see how he's feeling?"

He patted the top of her head. "The pay-off?" he asked Pop.

"Ten dollars."

"Fat chance!"

Julie put her hand on his arm. "Please, Mr. McCleary . . ."

She was looking up at him with magic blue eyes. "But, Julie—"

"Please . . ." she repeated softly.

He found his hand coming out of his pocket with a handful of bills. It was too late then. Pop's eyes were devouring the greenbacks.

"To your mother," said Lance sourly and began a reluctant count. "One—two—three— Let's see that ticket again."

He examined it closely, tossed it on the desk and continued, ". . . Four—five—six—seven—eight— That's all I—"

"Sufficient, Lance, my lad." Pop grabbed the money. "Keep the frame!"

He fled from the office.

"He forgot the ticket," said Julie.

Lance grinned. The old reprobate . . . Just the same he had warmed, as he always did, to the repeated, "Lance, my lad." When he was copy boy, it was an honor to have the great Farnsworth call him that, bliss to be noticed, and more, spoken to as an equal. The great man had taken Lance under his wing; and with a rush the boy had put him on a pedestal of hero worship and laid his love at his idol's feet. And deep in his heart the adult knew he had never taken it back . . .

Was there still a spark left in Pop of the Farnsworth who had rollicked through Europe interviewing kings and ministers with impious brutality, caught the first boat out of Liverpool to escape prison—and tore the heart of a nation with his personal story of the sinking of the Titanic?

Poor Pop . . . The bottle had always been his mistress; but one day he married it, and he didn't believe in divorce. But if it were taken away from him, could he, a gay and seasoned veteran, ever return to his place in newsdom as one of its most pungent headliners?

Lance thought of Pop mooching, staggering through City Hall Park, sleeping on a bench behind Civic Virtue, searching for gin-drops in the empties scattered along Frankfort Alley—and sighed.

Julie was looking up at him, smiling. "You really love that old man, don't you?" she said softly.

He jammed his hands in his pockets. "You owe me eight bucks."

"Oh, Mr. McCleary."

"Don't 'Oh, Mr. McCleary' me. How could you fall for that line of—for his line? You know he's an orphan."

"So do you."

"You hypnotized me!" He picked up the pawn ticket, dropped it into her palm. "Souvenir—eight bucks' worth."

Her chin came up angrily. "If that's all that's bothering you—don't worry, you'll get them back!"

"You bet I will. 'Oh, Mr. McCleary' has a long memory." He stamped out, muttering, "Roping me in—"

But late that afternoon, he blessed the eight dollars.

"What an investment," he gloated. "Wait'll I show Carl—boy, wait'll I show Carl!"

He swaggered through the city room making as much noise as he could. No head was raised. He strode to the desk where Carl was balancing art in the dummy spread before him and looked about disgustedly. Rabble . . . *You're too good for this paper, McCleary.*

"If you're sure I've had enough of the McCleary profile—" snapped Carl.

My best audience. "I've got the killer of Lonely Heart," Lance announced loudly.

"Where?"

"Right here at the city desk!"

Thirteen

It's a trap!

What's he got on me? Is he waiting for me to make a slip? He's all excited. He *has* got something. That's impossible. *But there's no one with him.* Don't be ridiculous. He's pulled that entrance before. He *thinks* he's got something. Even so, it's not like him to—What shall I do? There's only one thing I can do. I'm not supposed to know anything. He came in and told me he nailed the killer. That's big! It's dynamite. I'm supposed to get excited.

"*Where?*"

Lance lifted his arm in an arc and brought a suitcase down on the desk with a crash. All heads jerked up.

A suitcase? Is that all? But it must be important. Whose is it? Could it be *hers?* Where did he get it? Wait—I mustn't relax.

"What in hell's going on here?" he roared.

Lance clicked the latch and threw the suitcase open with a flourish. He was in his element. "Papa got a rattle for baby!"

Why doesn't he get right to it? Why does he have to be sensational? The phone on his desk rang. He reached for it still looking up at Lance. *If he's putting on an act, I have nothing to be afraid of.*

Someone was blubbering faintly into the other end of the line. A man. "Carl?"

"Yes."

"I'm sorry, Carl." *A familiar voice. Whose?* "Don't be angry, please don't be angry."

Oh—Pop Farnsworth. "What do you want?"

Pop sniveled and groaned. "I've a confession to make. I'm plunged into sorrow." His whisky cough tore into Carl's ears. ". . . added a nail to my coffin . . ."

"Get to the point!"

Pop whimpered. "Your tone—so sharp . . . Don't blame you. I took the ticket."

Ticket? So that's where it was. Pop had it all the time. But how? Pop was no thief . . . Of course— when he had given him the bill. It must have been crumpled with it . . .

". . . when you gave me the money." Pop choked over his words. "Must be forgiven . . . Want to buy you a drink . . . want to buy Lance a drink . . . I'm a miserable scoundrel. You must help me with Lance . . . I'm at Keene's. Bring Lance . . . You'll get your ticket back . . . Want to buy you a drink . . ."

Carl replaced the receiver slowly. *Why couldn't the ticket have been lost?*

He jerked a thumb at the suitcase. "Well?"

Lance picked something out of the jumble of clothes, held it out triumphantly. "There they are— Mr. and Mrs. Lonely Heart!"

It was a picture faded to a yellowish brown . . .

They had passed a concession at Revere Beach . . . "Fifty cents, have your picture taken, fifty cents." They had posed in front of the photographer's flivver; he had made a prop of it, hanging a Just Married sign across, tying old shoes and cans to the rear bumper. They had laughed at that.

She was smiling up at him. Her profile was unmistakable. But he did not know himself. The photographer had turned him three-quarter view; he had worn a mustache then and the peak of his Beau Brummel fedora threw a shadow across his face . . .

It *is* her suitcase . . . "Where'd you get this?"

"Julie's curiosity got the better of her and she went down to the hockshop."

"Make sense."

Lance told him about Pop.

That's why the old man's on a crying jag. He's not worried about the ticket; he's worried about Lance's eight dollars. Oh Pop, you should have been satisfied with that quarter . . . "Did he tell you where he got the ticket?"

"Nah. He stuck to that line about his old lady until he nabbed my eight bucks."

Lance is excited. I don't blame him. Too bad we're not in on this together—cold . . . Carl phoned the reference department. "Bring me all the pictures on Lonely Heart . . ." Whey they were brought to him he compared the photographs . . . "Yes, that's she."

"Sure it's her. A profile doesn't change."

"Who's he?"

"Her husband. It adds up. Old shoes—Just Married . . ." Lance picked up the picture and studied it as if it were the first time he had seen it.

Look at him, playing Sherlock Holmes again.

"We'll see what he looks like when we blow him up," said Lance.

I should have thought of that. Carl took it from him. He saw his face blown up to 8x11, to 16x22 . . . No danger. Not a chance of being recognized. He tossed it on the desk.

"See the license plate?" said Lance. "Barely make it out. Twenty and two letters—'s' and 's'. We know she comes from Mass. Throw it together and what we got? They were married in Massachusetts in 1920." He struck a new pose. "How's Papa doing?"

"You're feeding the baby the right kind of milk." Lance took it as sweet applause and waited for more. "But where's your killer?"

"The husband."

"How do you make that out?"

"Wedding ring."

"Meaning what?"

"He pulled it off—after he killed her. That's why it's gone."

It came off easily . . . "How do you know she didn't pawn it?"

"That's all there was at the shop."

Weak, Lance, weak. "And of course that's the only one in New York."

"Look, Carl: O'Hanlon will tell you the ring was taken off recently."

"That's right; probably hocked it to get to the Ball."

"Will you stop it?" shouted Lance. "I know my hunches. I tell you the killer took it!"

"Why?"

"Because there was an inscription on it."

Smart boy. "Got your crystal ball with you?"

"Don't tell me I'm not right. What about the ring you gave Mrs. Chapman? I'll bet *it* has an inscription."

To Rose from Carl, with love. *To Charlotte from John, with love.* Easy now. Look what you're doing— tearing off the corner of the dummy . . . "You're thinking like a legman!"

Lance reacted pugnaciously, ready to argue. But Carl went on. "You and your hunches. Wedding rings. Husbands. It's twenty years since that picture was taken. He may be dead. Maybe he's been married six times since then. Maybe he's the two-headed boy at Coney Island. *You* want him to be the killer—so he's the killer. McCleary waves his magic wand and the husband trots right into the *Comet* to fill page one."

Lance flushed. "Can you top it?"

"Sure I can top it! Where did Pop get the ticket?"

"He may have found it."

" 'He may have found it.' Go write for a true story magazine." He didn't like that. Now, again. "Use your head, Lance."

Ah—he's getting it. Look at his eyes begin to shine

. . . Lance smacked his forehead. "Holy smoke! *The killer!*"

"Now we're getting somewhere. Where did Pop get the ticket?" He made it dramatic. "Somebody gave it to him. Of course he didn't find it. If he did he wouldn't have left it behind. He'd have taken it with your money. But there was a reason why he left it. It's simple. Was he drunk when you saw him?"

"He was doing all right."

"That's it. The killer—" Carl felt a rising exhilaration. "Let's say I'm the killer. I have the ticket and I'm afraid to walk into the shop with it. Why? Because I don't know what she pawned. Maybe something that could identify me with her. I'm afraid to ask. I'm desperate. I've got to do something. I hang around the shop, trying to figure out a way without arousing any suspicion. Then Pop comes along. A bum. He asks me for a handout, and I get a bright idea. My way out. I give him some money to go into the shop with the ticket. But he forgets the shop once he has some money. You know how quickly Pop can disappear. He drinks up the money. Now he's in a spot. He sees a chance to raise cash on it. First Julie. Then you. But by this time he's suspicious. Why didn't the man want to go into the shop? Pop's an old hand—knows all the tricks. He knows the ticket is hot. He feels it. It isn't kosher. He doesn't want to have anything to do with it. He wants to sleep on park benches, not in the can. So he drops it quick. He leaves it on Julie's desk."

Lance's eyes were glued to him. "Find Pop—find the killer!"

I've got him going. I'll be able to get rid of him. "What's his favorite hangout?"

"Humpty O'Dollar's on Fourteenth."

"Start there and work down to the Bowery. Don't miss a dive. Find Pop and Madison'll drop a bonus in your lap. Get going."

"Gone!" Lance hurried out of the city room.

Carl pulled the dummy toward him. Ten minutes . . . I'll wait ten minutes.

He marked off two columns for a plane crash. Something jarred. What was it? That airline ad; it was right next to it. He riffled through the dummy to page twenty-one, measured the lines, drew one, wrote "airline crash."

The composing room foreman phoned. "We're tight. Keep it down."

He marked three sticks from China to overset. He had to squeeze that D.A.R. luncheon in somewhere. He found room for it in the second section.

Five minutes . . . He looked out the window; it was getting dark. He saw the picture in detail: the waterfront, the docks, the river . . .

Three minutes. He switched a restaurant ad next to the Broadway column, remembering a promise.

"I'm at Keene's."

It wasn't far; on South, across from the fish markets. He even knew which dock would be the only witness. Keene's was a block from the river. It had a big front window, a bar near by. He would tap on the window and Pop would come out and they'd walk off together to the dock, laughing and drinking.

Two minutes. He would rise and take his hat and

go out for a walk and kill an old man. In his mind he walked from Keene's to the dock . . . The dock, the river . . .

He pushed his chair back and took his hat off the tree and walked out of the city room. He passed the elevator and walked down cement stairs.

He pushed the glass door out, passed the cigar stand in the foyer and went toward South. Even walking there was easy. He was being taken to Keene's by a force that understood him, that wanted to help him.

South Street was quiet. A moon was coming up and he could smell fish and the river. Waterfront factories were quiet and dark. He passed an old woman poking around in the garbage near one of the markets; a cat gnawing at a hunk of refuse. He saw the stern light of a tug hauling a line of loaded barges. He paused in front of a big plate glass window upon which was crudely painted: *Keene's*.

Pop was leaning against the bar, hunched over a half-filled bottle and weeping into his glass. Carl tapped on the window.

Pop looked up, nodded, swooped the bottle to his breast and came out. He grabbed at Carl's lapel with his free hand. "Am I forgiven?" he blubbered.

Carl led him down the street. Pop hummed and swayed as he walked, leaning on Carl with his full weight. It didn't matter. Drunks lurching along the river were no novelty. They passed one sprawled out in a warehouse doorway.

Pop slumped in a heap. Carl glanced up and down the street. This neighborhood was paradise for lush-workers. There was no cop. There were only the snores from the slob in the doorway and a moan from the tug. A new shadow was thrown on the ground. Carl looked over his shoulder. It was his own. The moon was over Brooklyn Bridge now. He pulled Pop up.

"Come on," he said; "you want to buy Lance a drink, don't you?"

Pop's eyes were closed as he shook his head. His mouth opened and sputum ran down his chin. "Lance's my lad."

"Take a drink."

Pop took one and wiped his chin with the back of his hand. "Had to confess," he said. Then recalling why, he burst into tears again. "Gave Lance the ticket . . . I'll get it back . . . Spent his eight dollars . . . Have to help me, Carl . . ."

He trembled, tottered around Carl making a zig-zag circle and lurched against him. "Where's the bottle?"

"Right in your hand." They were approaching the dock.

Pop took a deep drink. "Got to save some for Lance. It's bonded."

"He's waiting for us."

Suddenly Pop jerked free. "Don't try to hold me back! Don't try to keep me from my lad." He waved the bottle majestically. "Let us proceed . . ."

Carl had to use his strength to keep him from sliding to the ground again as they walked under the dock. It was the dock he had chosen from behind his desk. Pop fell back against one of the piles and slid slowly to the ground, belching.

"Where's the bottle?" He found it in his lap and chuckled. Then a fresh flood of tears poured down his cheeks. "Lance'll be angry. Got to straighten it out for me, Carl." He stopped sobbing to cough. "Lance's my lad," he sang hoarsely. He tilted the bottle . . . "Good God—it's happened!" He was terrified. "Something's wrong, Carl. I'm sick. I can't swallow!"

"The cork."

"Oh." Pop tittered foolishly, pulled the cork out with his teeth and spat it out. "In the way all the time ——you!" He drained the bottle and began to whimper. "No more . . . no more for Lance . . ."

His head fell on his chest. His eyes closed and he mumbled to himself, still clutching the bottle.

Carl watched him. He could kick him in the head and drag him to the water and hold his head under— but drunks were hard to kill that way. He could strangle him. No; he couldn't touch him with his hands. On the ground were rocks. He could use that big one near Pop's feet. One swift blow and it would be over. His fingers ached. He looked down and saw them twitching and gripping the moist air.

He listened again; Pop's breathing was heavy, irregular. He found himself walking on tiptoe to something beyond the pile. It was an iron pipe, rusty and heavy. It was better than a rock; something to grip. A rock would be clumsy. He picked it up. His thumb closed over his fingers around the pipe. It was solid, long enough. He tiptoed back to Pop and stood in front of him. He pushed the old fedora off Pop's head. One good blow and it would be over.

He lifted the pipe and again heard the moan from

the tug and saw it as an illustration for a story: tugboat; barges; dirty river; bridge; moon; a drunk;
and a man standing over him with a pipe in his fist.
He brought the pipe down—

No! Not this way! His hand was frozen above him.
He locked his teeth against shouting. I can't do this!
I can't! Not this way. I can't. I'm sick. I'm going to
vomit. I can't kill him! I was wrong. It isn't easy. I
can't do it. It's not right. It's too cold. It's wrong. It's
crazy. I'm not crazy. I'm not mad. I can't do this. I
can't. I can't—

He brought the pipe down just as Pop's head tilted
back against the pile. It smashed the jaw. Pop groaned.
His eyes opened and rolled. He gurgled.

No! No! I can't go on!

You can't stop now. Hard. Hard! He brought the
pipe down on the head, hard.

He was breathing heavily. His fingers were grown
to the pipe. The skull had been bashed down to the
cheekbones. He lifted his arm and hurled the pipe.
It left his fingers easily. There was a splash. The light
from the tugboat winked. It was passing Dover Street
now.

He turned without looking back and walked. He
crossed South. The same old woman. The cat was
gone. Two sailors stumbled out of a quiet saloon on
Roosevelt. He turned the corner. There down the
block, closing the dead-end street, was the *Comet*
building . . .

He stopped and took off his hat. The breeze was
cool. He closed his eyes and drew a deep breath.

It *is* easy . . .

He lit a cigarette. His hands were trembling. But that was natural. The trembling stopped. He flipped away the match and went on. How good the cigarette tasted . . .

He entered the *Comet* building. In the washroom, he washed his hands thoroughly, dried them with the cheap newsprint used as towels. He went to his desk, hung his hat on the tree and sat down.

The proofs of the more legible format and new type dress he had ordered were ready for him. He glanced at the editorial, called in the composing room foreman.

He listened to his own criticism. It was brief and expert. "I told you to stick to that new body type. This editorial is still eight-point Paragon on nine-point base. Sure there's plenty of space between the lines, but I never want to see an editorial again in eight point."

The phone rang. Madison, to thank him for his advice on the defamation of character suit. It had been dropped.

He hung up. He knew it would be. Madison was so easily hysterical.

A young reporter, fresh out of journalism school, came up with an item: A religious woman who could "prove by the Bible that salt water'll take the ticks off'n sheep" was outside with one.

"With one what?"

"With a sheep. She's got a bottle of salt water. I think she's crazy, Mr. Chapman. She followed me back to the office."

"Probably a character actress for that new show.

All right; have Biddle get a shot of her and we'll run it so you can get a couple of tickets."

The reporter flushed, stammered. "I'm sorry, Mr. Chapman, I—I tried—"

"Forget it. Only in the future don't try to mix publicity with work."

The reporter slunk away.

Carl studied the assignment sheet. Lance had not got back yet.

Fourteen

On the low flat steps of soot-stained City Hall, Lance stretched his long legs before him, leaned back on his elbows, and watched the kids still splashing each other in the Civic Virtue fountain.

He felt no guilt loafing on the steps. He was in love with doing nothing. He had several straight ryes in him and he was mellow and lazy.

Maybe you're not such a jackass after all, Lance, m'boy, letting Carl send you out on an asinine search for Pop. This is worth it. So help me, he ought to be a director. He had me playing Trilby to his Svengali. No, he ought to be an actor. That speech about Pop and the killer! I fell for it—me, McCleary—until I got outside. Then it hit me. Yep, that's when. But do I get sore and tear back to raise hell? Not me. I go and toy with some drinks and here I be. That "toy" is good.

No, he ought to be writing detective stories. Can you imagine a killer smart enough to murder and get away with it, cunning enough to remove all marks of identification and set the stage for an accident, taking that damning evidence of a pawn ticket and just handing it over neatly to gin-soaked Pop? Just to make it nice for us. For pulps he ought to be writing!

Of course Pop found the ticket! But just because the big editor's got an imagination, I'm supposed to cover fifty thousand slophouses in this town and put my finger on the old man—*ptt!* like that. What am I —Superman?

He got out a pencil, slid down a little and snuggled his shoulder blades against the steps until he found the perfect position.

Let's see—"Cap'n" Dickey's cab to Humpty O'Dollar's on Fourteenth . . . He shut his eyes and enjoyed the ride.

Cab to Humpty's—60¢, he listed virtuously, peering at the folded copy paper through the growing dark. He muttered, "Keep the change, Cap," and added: 15¢ tip.

He settled down to some fancy robbery. Cab to Lafayette & Howard—40¢. What, would you cheat an honest working man? He changed it to 65¢ inc. tip.

Cab to Rivington and Orchard—50¢ and 50¢ tip. Fifty cents for a tip? Sure. Hadn't the driver told him he had seen Pop around Pell and Mott?

He pondered: without patting himself on the back, it might be said he had an unparalleled talent for investigation. He had proven it. Investigation was a challenge. But trying to find Pop in some Bowery gin-mill wasn't—it was stupid. It was an insult. He resented it.

It cost the *Comet* exactly seventy cents for phantom phone calls. Itemized drinks for imaginary bums who thought they knew Pop's whereabouts brought the figure up to $5.80. Satisfied with this petty larceny, he stuffed pencil and paper into his pocket, rested on his elbows again and yawned . . .

Ah, McCleary, you were born too late . . . What a help you'd have been to Greeley or Bennett. Sure you would have worn a paper collar, striped shirt, black derby and maybe even carried a cane. But you'd have blasted the Tweed Ring, scribbled captions for Tom Nast's cartoons and handled editorials for *Harper's Weekly*, on the side . . .

You'd be Greeley's right-hand man; and when he invited all libel suits to keep his *Tribune* alert, you'd tell him he was making a big mistake. "Oh," he'd say, "you don't agree with me, Lance?" And you'd say, with dignity, "Nope, Horace, I don't."

It was better with a cigar. He lit a cigar. "Nope, Horace, I don't." Wasn't that stretching a point? He tried again. "No, Mr. Greeley, I don't."

That's how it would have been.

"McCleary, go find Livingstone."

"Where is he, Jim?"

"Somewhere in Africa."

"Sure, Jim." If young Bennett wanted you to find Livingstone, all right, you'd find him.

But you wouldn't have said, "Dr. Livingstone, I presume." Not you. Not the great McCleary. You'd have said, "I'm McCleary of the *Herald*." And you'd never have gone down to posterity . . .

Yup—there would be no newsreels to show you chartering a tug with three divers from Key West and finding proof that the *Maine* was sunk . . . McCleary goes down in a diver's suit and finds the *Maine* for the *World*. Not bad, not bad . . . Old Pulitzer would beg you to take a pleasure jaunt with him to the Mediterranean.

You'd be cock o' the walk . . . champagne at Mouquin's, dates at the Astor House, dinners at the Waldorf. During the day you'd be the Dostoievsky of Park Row, at night the dandy of New York. The idol of the press—McCleary—the swashbuckling reporter, smashing villains with a cobblestone fist, damning the wicked, protecting the weak—

Like hell you would. You haven't got what it takes. You had to be hard in those days. Tough and a gogetter like—well, like Pop. Now *there* was a newspaperman. Imagine the old drunk pulling a stunt like that when he was twenty and sober—boarding blind Pulitzer's yacht for a job and being hurled overboard. Did he give up? He crashed Pulitzer's cabin five minutes later, shouted for a job and got it.

Ah, Pop. "Lance, my lad, no newspaperman ever expunges the cloy of printer's ink from his nostrils." Didn't you, Pop?

But what a *real* swashbuckler! Five years on the *Globe* and a bellyful of Tolstoy and what does he want to do? Write classics! Did you ever want to write classics, McCleary? You did not. But Pop did. And of all the breaks—he gets there just in time to see Father Gapon and his petitioners shot down by the hundreds outside the Winter Palace in St. Petersburg. Did he forget Tolstoy? Sure he did. He got drunk, and came back on the *Globe* with an eye-witness description of the massacre.

That was a story!

He stretched his arms. Ho-hum—what a day. He took a deep breath of the sacred air. It was the same air they had breathed, those great newspapermen. And what are you, McCleary? A call boy for a drunk!

He rose and stamped his feet. They had fallen asleep. It was getting chilly. The rye had worn óff. Coffee would help.

He passed a hoarse preacher who had chalked up the sidewalk with messages from God in front of the statue of Benjamin Franklin, and went into the Park Row Café.

Its chairs looked ready to give way, the tables were patched together. Only the counter looked modern. It had been installed the day Peary reached the North Pole. He seated himself at a corner table. "Coffee."

"Ho-kay, Mac," said the counterman. "Say, you got a nice rye look. Cream?"

"Lancelot McCleary!"

Lance turned. Old Man Sweeney, owner of the café, was hobbling eagerly over to his table. Ninety and stubborn as a dike, he always said he'd open another café when he reached the century mark. He might, at that. "Hello, Johnny."

" 'Bout time you showed up!" Sweeney skidded, grabbed the corner of the table and lowered himself by degrees into the chair opposite; Lance knew better than to help him. "Ain't seen much of you 'round here. Where you been?"

Lance thought quickly. "Been eating in," he said. "How you doing?"

Sweeney screwed his face into the grin caricatured

by all New York's cartoonists. "I'm gonna outlive all you boys." He cackled. "I started makin' java when I was fifteen an' I'll keep on a-makin' it when you're all dead-'n-gone. I'm the best java-maker on Park Row."

"Anything with the coffee, Mac?" asked the counterman.

"A bear's claw," said Lance.

Sweeney snorted and banged the table. "Nothin' doin'! We got a plate o' corned beef 'n cabbage tonight that proves Dinty Moore got English blood in him!"

"Ho-kay?" asked the counterman.

"Ho-kay."

Sweeney put his elbows on the table and leaned on them. "They workin' you hard, boy?"

"I'm a slave," said Lance.

"Huh; you don't know what workin' is. Why back in the days . . ."

It was coming. The saga of the Park Row Café was going to be retold and reenacted. Lance had heard it some thirteen years, it had been run as a perennial feature story in one paper or another; he enjoyed it every time. He had never had the courage to interrupt the old man—but then, he never wanted to.

". . . from dawn to dawn," Sweeney was saying. "You don't know what tired is. But I didn't mind. The things I seen an' heard, Lancelot."

Lance knew a moment of envy.

"Did I ever tell you about that night back in July, '63?"

Lance shook his head. "I don't think you did."

"Well, it was about ten o'clock—Give Lancelot plenty o' them boiled spuds!"

"Ho-kay."

"—durin' the Draft Riots. Bad boys, them rioters . . . bad."

The counterman placed the order before Lance and tiptoed away.

"They'd got after the nigger orphan asylum—" Sweeney shoved the mustard across the table to Lance, "an' burned it down. Right to the ground. Then they headed this way."

His eyes were fixed eerily on the door; Lance, watching him, stopped chewing. "I saw 'em marchin' right into Printin' House Square . . ."

Lance saw them too, a thousand of them, singing, "We'll hang old Greeley to a sour apple tree and send him straight to Hell!"

"Be careful with that mustard, boy. I made it . . . They was yellin' they was goin' to burn the *Tribune!*"

Sweeney waited. "Did they get into the building?" asked Lance.

"*Get* in? They *smashed* in. An' you know what they done?"

"They set it on fire!"

"That's what they done. Smoke come right through that window." Sweeney pointed. "Me? I was washin' dishes then an' cleanin' grill. The smoke fit to make me cough to death."

He coughed, overcome. ance pushed his water glass toward him. "Thanks, Lancelot. An' then you know what happened?"

"No—what?"

"The back door busts open—an' who comes flyin' in here—but *Horace Greeley!* Hear that, boy? Horace Greeley!"

"No! The old man himself?"

"That's who!"

"What'd he do?"

"He didn't wait a minute. He ducked under this table—right under this here table, Lancelot!"

"Wow!"

"He hid right where your feet are." Lance moved his feet. "He was sweatin' an' scared. 'Save me, Johnny, save me!' he says."

"And did you?"

"O-ho, did I? There was me, master of the situation. 'I'll save you, Mr. Greeley,' I says. An' just a second before them Bowery boys busts in, I whips off a tablecloth," Sweeney whipped an imaginary cloth from the table, "an' I throwed it over him!"

"And they didn't find him!"

"They didn't. Me, Johnny Sweeney, I saved him from bein' swung!"

He leaned back, panting.

"What a night!" said Lance. "I don't think I could have stood it." But the story wasn't finished. "Was he grateful?"

Sweeney was. "Not him. He'd come in here an' sit where you're sittin' an' drink his coffee an' pretend like nothin' happened."

"It's the same coffee," muttered Lance.

"You'd think he'd give me a subscription for life to his paper, wouldn't you?"

"Sure I would."

"Well, no such thing. I still had to plunk down my two cents every time I bought a *Tribune!* How about a piece of pie?"

"Couldn't hold it. Johnny, would you like a life subscription to the *Comet?*"

Sweeney licked his lips. "You mean it?" He put out his hand. "Put 'er there, Lancelot."

They shook hands solemnly.

"Any time *you* get into trouble like that," Sweeney jabbed a leathery finger at the air in the direction of Lance's nose. "*You* come to me too!"

"I will," promised Lance.

He left the café in a glow the rye could not have given him . . .

Outside the *Comet*, the pressroom plank was up; they were rolling newsprint into the basement. News trucks were backed up to the loading platform, their drivers circled around a hot crap game. He stopped to look on. Mechanically his hand went to his pocket; but he resisted. He went on, smug in the thought that he could turn his back successfully on temptation. Jackson of the pressroom waved a paper-hook as he passed.

He went up to the city room whistling. In the wire room a bell clanged a "must"; one of the copy boys hurried in and ripped the story from the teletype machine. Most of the rewrites were busy. Lights were blazing over the art department and Monroe in the slot was checking names from the *Who's Who*.

The same old routine . . . Ah, yes, McCleary, you *were* born too late. The glow faded. You're just another reporter destined to end up on the copy desk or playing poker with rookies at police headquarters.

"Where's Mr. Chapman?" he asked a boy.

"In photo."

Lance went down the corridor and met Carl just coming out of the photo room.

"Bring him with you?" said Carl. "Who gave it to him?"

"Couldn't find him."

"That's bad. He's liable to run into the killer again."

"For the love of Mike, Carl, I couldn't look in the alleys too! He's probably sleeping it off in one of them."

"Well, never mind now. You're just in time. I can use you. You like to mug. Come on."

Lance followed him back into the photo room. There, the rubicund Amos Biddle was not allowing business to interfere with pleasure. He was trying to date a pretty, giggling girl, one of the secretaries from the advertising department. He looked doleful at the interruption.

"Set up?" said Carl. Biddle grunted and got behind the camera. "I've got somebody who's ham enough to give us a good performance." Carl turned to Lance. "We're shooting the murder of Lonely Heart. You're the killer."

Lance was bored. Old stuff, a composite. They'd paste Lonely Heart's head on the girl's body, cut out his face and replace it with a question mark. He sniffed. "There's a funny smell here."

"Sheep," said Carl. "Ready, Biddle?" The cameraman was ogling the girl. "Biddle!"

"Yeah, boss!"

Carl moved the girl into position in front of a drab-gray drop. "Stand in front of her, Lance. Now, Tina, dig your nails into his hair. And Lance, I want your arm out, coming around to hit her." He stepped back. "Can you see her fingers in his hair, Biddle?"

"Got it."

"Strike her, Lance," said Carl. "No, not like that. Make it look real. Here—watch me."

Lance watched him fake a right to Tina's jaw and shook his head. I wouldn't punch like that. But why worry? It's *his* show . . . He stepped before the camera and faked a right.

"Got it," said Biddle.

"Fall, Tina," ordered Carl. "Go on, fall!" Tina dropped. "Got it," said Biddle.

"Now hold your head up a few inches, Tina, as if you—" Carl looked around, took a small cardboard box from a shelf and put it on the floor. "Rest your head on that and look dead."

"Got it," said Biddle.

"That's all, Tina," said Carl. "Thanks. Collins!" A man wearing a rubber apron came out of the dark room. Biddle gave him the plates. "Bring those in as soon as they're ready," Carl ordered. "Come on, Lance."

Lance followed him out and down the corridor. Carl paused to drink at the fountain near the phone booth.

A short slight man appeared behind him. "Hello, Mr. Chapman," he said when Carl straightened and wiped his mouth. "I'm Swan. Just off the San Diego

Sun. They folded. Shainmark told me to mention him."

"What did you do?"

"On the rim."

"See Monroe."

"Thanks."

In the news room Carl put out his hand. "Let's have it."

Lance dropped his swindle sheet on the desk, watched Carl out of the corner of his eye.

"Fifty cents for a tip?" asked Carl. "What for?"

"The driver told me he saw Pop around Pell and Mott." Didn't catch me on that one. I was prepared . . .

Carl scribbled an okay on the sheet. "That rape fiend was finally caught—a shoe clerk from Canarsie." He gave Lance the story. "Yerkes muffed on it. You're supposed to be perspicacious. Prove it."

Lance's eyebrows went up. "Last month it was perspicuous."

He started for his desk. Coster, the picture editor, stopped him. "There was a phone call for you, Lance."

That dinner date with Julie!

"It was Dr. O'Hanlon."

O'Hanlon? "What did he want?"

"It's about Pop Farnsworth. They just picked him up near the river. Someone bashed his head in. He's down at the Morgue now."

Coster returned to his table. Lance looked after him in a daze. He turned to Carl. "What'd he say?"

"Pop's dead. Killed. I *told* you to find him."

Killed? Pop killed? Head bashed in? The *Morgue?*

"Poor miserable souse," murmured Carl.

Who'd want to kill Pop? Who'd want to hurt that old— The ticket! That goddam ticket! Carl *was* right. It's the same killer . . . He got away with it once— but he's not going to get away with it this time. He's not going to get away with it this time. I've got to get him. I'll get him.

He lost control. "I'll get that rat if it's the last thing I do!"

Fifteen

So he's going to get me . . .

He's so young, so determined, so emotional. I didn't know he cared for the old man that much. Too bad it had to be Pop . . .

"Well, what are you waiting for?" Carl said. "Call the Morgue, get the details. He was a drunk but it's still murder."

Wait a minute . . . there's something in this. I can't put my finger on it. A new angle . . . How can I use it?

Suddenly the old excitement gripped him. He saw the lead, the follow-up . . . He would splash it in red and black, the redder the better. Had he had this idea all the time or had it just come in a prescient flash? He didn't know.

He heard himself say, "Hold it." It was hard to keep his voice even.

Lance was waiting. Carl ran his eyes over the boys at their desks: Prindle was on politics, Gibson on sleeping sickness, Payne on divorce, Rogers on theft —"Rogers."

An unfriendly caricature of a typical Yankee unhitched himself from his typewriter and strolled to the desk. Carl held out a hand to Lance. "I'll take that."

"Rehash this," he told Rogers. "Dig up stuff on Jack the Ripper and Vacher. Make comparisons between them and this shoe clerk."

Rogers nodded and took the shoe clerk back with him.

Carl smiled at Lance. "Well, your baby's crawling." Lance looked blank. "Pop," said Carl.

"I don't get it."

"From now on Pop and Lonely Heart are Siamese twins."

Lance frowned. "What are you going to do, bury *him* too?"

"No, *run* him."

"On what?"

"Imagination."

"I'll take castor oil."

"Or the 'Canons of Journalism' for your birthday!" said Carl sarcastically.

"So I'm sentimental!" flared Lance. "But—damn it, this is *Farnsworth*."

Still a hero worshiper, at his age. He makes me feel so gray . . . "And we're making him a great newshawk who died in harness—who gave his life for a story."

"Loud cheers."

I'll put a stop to this. "Get off the soapbox!" He saw the effect of his voice on Lance.

Lance shrugged. "All right, I'm off." He conceded grudgingly. "What's your slant?"

On a sheet of copy paper Carl scribbled: "LONELY

HEART SLAYER STRIKES AGAIN!" and shoved
it at Lance. "That's what we're going to sell. The rest
is easy. Pop got the ticket and gave it to you. He was
suspicious. The eight bucks never happened. You
went down to the pawnshop, came back with her
suitcase. The picture tied Pop right up with the killer.
We told him to dig. He was an old newspaperman, the
best of his era. He dug and came up with a clue leading to the apprehension of the killer—but he was
bashed in the head before he got to the office. Pop's a
hero, I'm a genius, you're a wonder boy, the readers
are happy, the members are thrilled, and the cops
want to cut our throats."

Lance had to try twice before he could speak. "Of
all the crazy things I ever heard! How are you going
to make it stick?"

"Simple. Pop phoned."

"Phoned who? When?"

"Me. He got the dope and phoned me, telling me
he was on his way up with it. The killer overheard and
that was that."

Lance scratched his chin. "Yeah, that'll work. No,
wait, there's a flaw. Maybe he was rolled."

"Plant dough on him."

Lance shook his head. "You don't miss a trick."

"Are you still in this room," said Carl, "or do you
want me to write it myself?" He picked up the phone,
called circulation. "What's the run?"

"Seven-forty-five."

"Make it seven-sixty-five." He hung up. "If we
don't jump twenty thousand with this yarn," he told
Lance, "I'll eat your hat."

"You're the boss," said Lance. "I'll have baby on roller skates before I'm through. Only it's your baby now."

"Here's your line-up: Stolen pawn ticket bares Lonely Heart's marriage. Dean of reporters slain on way to *Comet* to reveal killer."

"Put it to music and you'll have an anthem for the club." Lance turned on his heel.

But Carl was satisfied. Lance was sour. The story would sparkle. He lined up page one. Two columns for the picture of "Mr. and Mrs. Lonely Heart."

Mr. and Mrs. Lonely Heart . . . He remembered his qualms about Charlotte and he could have laughed aloud. He relished again the story he was manufacturing, the machine he was setting in motion . . . He was the potent hub. When before had the man with the green eyeshade such a run? Always the editor recorded; could only rely on rumor and believe an eyewitness; was only an echo of action. But he was different. To the average editor, to any editor, this would be a nightmare. But not to him. He felt himself tower over the men in the news room. He looked about, savoring his own omnipotence.

"Lance," he called, "don't forget the picture from the suitcase. Go heavy on the husband angle."

"That part's the only thing that makes sense," came back Lance. "He's the killer or I'll eat *your* hat!"

You won't have to . . . Carl measured off two columns for the photo, wrote the caption himself: DO YOU RECOGNIZE THIS MAN? HE IS LONELY HEART'S HUSBAND. THE COMET

WILL PAY $5,000 TO ANYONE WHO CAN IDENTIFY HIM.

He could imagine Madison, "Five thousand? Have you lost your mind? Have you gone—"

And himself, "If he's identified, I'll pay the reward myself."

Lance's copy would be just enough for a flash; not even enough for a jump. Color, a boxed extra. Collins, from the dark room, spread the drying photos for the composite in front of him. Carl saw startling scenes of violence caught by Biddle's lens.

He called the tall head of the art department to his desk and pointed. "That's one, that's two, that's three, that's four."

"I'll have the first rough in about twenty minutes, Mr. Chapman."

Lance's fingers were flying over his keys; he was still wearing the expression of an executioner. Carl chuckled. He gave a boy the bannerline he had written. "Take this down to fudge. Wait for the proof."

The boy left. What was Lance doing with that story? "You writing a novel?"

Lance ripped the copy out of his machine and brought it to him. The lead was perfect, as Carl had known it would be. But Lance was pale.

"Sick?"

"Headache," said Lance.

"Take an aspirin."

"Forget it." Lance walked out of the news room.

Carl read the story, found it flawless, shot it into the composing room. The composite layout of Lonely Heart's murder was brought to him. He studied it.

"Your continuity is all wrong. Picture one is him striking her; two is digging her nails into him; three she falls; four she's dead. Paint a row of arrows to the bathroom. Plant a copy of the *Comet*. Not enough air-brush here. I want the foot of the bed played up more."

Proofs were dumped on the desk. He hurried into the composing room with them, had his usual argument with the foreman. "Can't you get your boys to slug these right?" he exploded.

There was the usual alibi. He started back to his desk. He heard an operator call out, "Pick-up—Mc-Cleary."

Carl stood behind him, watched Lance's story flow through the linotype, raw, hot, shaping itself in molten metal . . . Lance has gone to the Morgue. He'll learn it was an iron pipe . . . He'll learn that Pop was so drunk he didn't know what hit him. That will make Lance feel better . . . Then *he'll* go out and get drunk.

What else will he find out? What else *can* he find out? Well, I'll wait and see . . .

But his threat? I wonder if that was just hysterics. I wonder if he meant it. Hysterics make headlines . . . That's good. I can use it. I can use that threat. I know it . . .

Of course I can use it! Lance, you're a godsend.

Sixteen

It was the first time Lance hated to go there. He had always been the outsider; now he felt like a relative.

The presses had begun to roll. He could feel their vibration through the sidewalk.

"Hi, Mr. McCleary."

A driver with the face of an English bull was leaning against a fender of his cab. He grinned hopefully. He was Lance's favorite hack.

"Hello, Cap."

Cap'n Dickey swung open the cab door. "You don't want to take the subway, Mr. McCleary."

"Okay, I don't." Lance climbed in. "Morgue."

"Somebody dead again?"

"Yes."

Cap ignored a red light. "I was tellin' the boys about how we went down an' found out that dame was murdered. They didn't believe me till they read it in the paper. I told them about the funeral too. Now they call me Joe Scoop." He guffawed. "Good, huh? This one a dame too?"

"No."

"Hey, that reminds me—" Cap remembered a new bawdy story he was sure Lance had not heard. He told it with gusto, lowering his voice genteelly on forbidden words. He was disappointed in Lance's reaction. "What'sa matter? Don't you feel good?"

"Headache."

"I bet it's your stomach. When I—"

"Come on, Cap, step on it."

"Oh, this one's a big shot, huh?"

When they pulled up with a screech at the Morgue, Lance said, "Stick around."

"You bet."

The interview with Dr. O'Hanlon was short. It left Lance feeling sick . . . When he came out, Cap said, "Hey, now you don't *look* good."

Lance told him to drive to the nearest bar. Cap fished hopefully. "Another murder?"

"Yes."

Cap peered back over his shoulder. "You ain't excited like last time. What'sa matter? Jeez, ain't a relative?"

"No."

"You don't act like you got a story, Mr. McCleary."

Lance said nothing. When he was paid off, Cap tried again. "Want I should stick around, huh?"

For the first time Lance smiled. "You're a good guy, Cap. But—no."

He pushed his way to the crowded bar, tossed a bill across it and got it back in rye. A girl snuggled up to him.

"Blue, mister?"

He ignored her and clung to his glass. He made a
bet with himself: the sixth drink would kill his headache. He lost . . .

Why was he getting drunk? He remembered. He
had lost a friend . . . He was alone in his grief. Of
all the people in New York there was no one to mourn
Pop. Only me . . . He took another drink. O'Hanlon
would understand. He called me, didn't he? It's a
shame he has to work. But that's how it is . . .

"Look, sister, I'm *not* blue. Peddle it somewhere
else."

You're in despair, McCleary. You ought to do
something about it. He thought deeply and came up
with four alternatives. He itemized them with pre-
cision:

1. *Get going.* He had threatened before Carl and
God to get Pop's slayer. Getting soused is a waste of
time, McCleary. It's an indication of mawkishness.

2. *Think.* What leads had he? He was like a magnet
when it came to leads. But there was nothing around.
Just a headache.

3. *Keep sober.* It had always been impossible to
tap a climax with liquor under his belt even when
he was well-informed. He needed a hunch; the rye
was delaying the birth.

4. *Get good and drunk.* Drunk—hunch . . . No,
they didn't rhyme. But it could be that after a bender
he could make them rhyme.

Number four was the best.

"No, sister, I haven't a match."

Make Pop a hero, that's what Carl said. And he's

right too. It gives Pop a swell exit even if it *is* phony. Me, I have to go moral and sound off like a high priest of journalism. He ought to have kicked me in the pants.

"No, sister, I don't know no Don Wiley."

But Carl should have set aside a special spot for Pop, an honor corner—all by itself; that's what he should have done. On the editorial page. Not too heavy a border.

"Say, bartender, got a typewriter?"

It was a small office. The machine was an old Royal; he patted it fondly. He poured himself a drink from a fresh pint and crouched over the typewriter.

A tribute—that's what this is going to be. He typed: "Pop is dead. The great Richard Farnsworth, whose blood and ink made newspaper history, is dead." He read that over. Now don't get maudlin, McCleary. Keep it simple. Concise. He banged the carriage to the right, went on: "The golden shower of matrices are his children, the roar of the presses are but the echoes of his voice . . ."

He finished, feeling sure this obituary would have delighted Pop, folded it affectionately and put it into an inside pocket. Then he took it out again. What about the honor corner on the editorial page? Why wait? There was a telephone on the desk. He used it to summon a messenger boy. He gave the boy the tribute and made him raise his right hand in solemn oath to deliver it into the hands of Carl Chapman himself and none other.

After that he stared at the machine and tried to

collect his thoughts. What was the next move he had planned? Oh yes, the bottle . . . His headache was worse. He was nauseous. He had to get out.

He prowled through the streets in an ugly mood, careened into a small bar, treated the tavern to a mass souse in the hope that generosity would cheer him. It didn't. Depressed, he made the rounds . . .

He came lurching out of a saloon and shoved through a crowd surrounding a wily little anti-tongued rabble-rouser. He always had hated rabble-rousers. He began to heckle with a ragged salvo of abuse. A few pro handclaps encouraged him to more direct pungency. The little orator raised his hand; the antis rushed Lance. He loved it . . . A burly anti kicked him. Lance slugged him twice. He was hit on the head and went down, swinging all the way.

Someone plunged through the melee and dragged him from the battleground.

"I been tailing you, Mr. McCleary," panted Cap Dickey. He brushed Lance off anxiously. "You okay?"

Lance lifted the driver's yellow cap and patted his square head. "Never touched me," he said and passed out.

He came to as he was being half-dragged, half-guided down a corridor. "Turkish bath?" he chirped.

"No, sir." Cap knocked on a door. "It's me—Cap Dickey," he called. "I'm with Mr. McCleary."

The door swung open. Julie stood there. "Hello, beautiful," said Lance.

She stared at him. "What happened?"

"Drunk," said Cap.

"Mr. McCleary!"

Lance pushed away from Cap and staggered past her into the apartment.

"I wouldn't have brung him here, Miss Allison," Cap was explaining worriedly, "except that all the way in my cab he kept yelling I should."

"I did not!" denied Lance hotly.

Cap was respectful but firm. "Yes, you did, Mr. McCleary."

"Didn't!" He turned to Julie. "Did I?" He collapsed on the divan and peered up at them through blurred eyes.

"Want I should take him home, Miss Allison?" asked Cap.

"No," declared Lance.

"Maybe we ought to try to get him more sober," said Julie.

He let them go to work on him with ice cubes and hot coffee . . . Finally Julie said, "I think he'll be all right now. How much does he owe you?"

"Aw, he'll see me tomorrow. Take it easy, Mr. McCleary."

Lance heard Julie say, "Thanks, Cap." The door closed.

When he opened his eyes she was standing over him. She looked so little and cute glaring down at him with her hands on her hips. She was wearing something blue with stripes; it had a bow that tied it at the waist. He reached for the bow. She slapped his hand away and began to lecture him roundly . . . the dinner date he had forgotten . . . getting drunk instead . . . his shameful condition . . . his brazenness . . .

She paused for breath. "Mr. McCleary, are you listening?"

"Yes, Julie."

"Then why don't you say something?"

"You're a cutie, Julie."

"I don't mean that."

"Got nothing else to say . . . Julie, I don't feel good."

Her attitude changed instantly. She put a tender hand on his forehead.

"You hear about Pop?" he asked.

She nodded, stroked his hair gently. "Is that why you got drunk?"

He wanted to say yes, but he knew that it would be a lie . . . He had to face it. He could avoid it no longer. "It's my fault!"

She sat beside him. "What is?"

Words flowed from him incoherently . . . his sullen brooding flared into profane self-accusation, startling her.

"What do you mean *you* killed him?" she said.

"I should have looked for him . . . Carl sent me out to look for him and what did I do? I was smart so I did nothing." He rose, steadying himself against the table. "I could have saved him. Go on, say it! I could have found him. Sure I could've. Carl warned me but I played wise guy. I did a lot of fancy nothing . . . And all the while Pop's hat is off and he's drunk and he doesn't see that iron pipe coming down . . ."

"Ah, don't." She led him back to the divan.

"Oh, Julie, I feel so—so . . ."

"I know, darling," she said. "You feel like crying."

She had called him darling instead of Mr. Mc-Cleary . . . Soft blackness was waiting for him. He wanted to sink into it. But he had to tell her something. It was important. "Julie, remind me to hide under a table," he managed to say. "Don't forget. Remind me . . ."

Sleep caught him so quickly that he heard his first snore . . .

It was a crisp morning. He hated it. Avoiding the sun, he walked to the corner café.

He caught a glimpse of himself in the mirror behind the coffee urn. He looked awful. He was bathed and shaved but he looked awful. This was one morning he shouldn't go to work. What he needed was peace and quiet and a comforting cool hand against his brow.

What would be waiting for him at the office—parricide? matricide? infanticide? fratricide? Or perhaps a poisoning before lunch, a garroting after and an unidentified skull in a crock to sharpen his appetite for dinner. He shuddered. Julie was right. He had had enough of murders, ax, hex and cult . . . enough of dismembered bodies in trunks, in closets, buried in gardens; he was fed up with arms in barrels and legs in boxes, bones in cement and guns in reservoirs. Why should he waste his youth being a clue chaser, digging up thrills for sensation-hungry morons, when he could be preparing himself for a loftier, a more respectable position?

"You don't have to cover crime to be a great newspaperman," she had said. He agreed with her. He could handle a column, cover ship news, makeup, write heads, rim or rewrite . . . a dozen jobs were his for the asking in the craft he loved. Crime wasn't the only thing he shone at. Yes, certainly Julie was right.

But after a pint of tomato juice spiked with Worcestershire, ham and eggs and three cups of coffee, she didn't know what she was talking about. He lit a cigar and wondered at himself—had that been Mc-Cleary about to desert crime for copy slashing?

He strutted to the *Comet,* enjoying the cigar and the morning with deep inhalations, and looked forward eagerly to a new day of horror, terror and thrills.

The newsboy around the corner handed him a fresh edition and caught the flipped coin in one practiced sweep. "Hope you get'm, Mr. McCleary."

"Thanks, son," said Lance benevolently. Then it occurred to him: Hope I get who?

He found the answer in the headline. He took one look at it and was on his way into the *Comet* building, up to the city room and through it to Carl's desk. He slammed the paper on the desk.

"This is a hell of a joke!"

Carl looked up and smiled. "How's the hangover?"

Lance thumped page one. "Never mind that—how about this?"

Unperturbed, Carl leaned back and rocked. "You went to the Morgue last night, didn't you?" he said amiably. "What'd you find?"

"Nothing. What about this publicity?"

"What was he hit with?"

"Iron pipe. Quit playing Legree, Carl."

"How do they know—they find it?"

"No. Crumbs of rust and metal filings in what was left of the head. He was so drunk he didn't know what hit him. This is a dirty trick!"

"What is?" asked Carl innocently. He leaned forward, glanced at the bannerline. To Lance it seemed to be the only type: "I'LL GET KILLER!" SWEARS REPORTER.

"Oh, that," said Carl. "Had to use something for replate."

"Replate first edition, eh? You were so stuck you had to dig up something strictly between you and me." Lance glared at the details. They were all there: his search for Pop and the hunt through the Bowery; his race against the unknown murderer; his failure to find Pop before the slayer of Lonely Heart; the dramatic interpretation of his oath "to get" the homicidal maniac who bludgeoned the head of his best friend, his idol . . .

"You're the big hero now," said Carl.

"I'm the patsy!" bellowed Lance. " 'Get off the soapbox!' That's a fine thing to tell me and then splash my speech all over town. You're making me a Rover Boy."

"You're taking it like one."

"It won't be our throats, it'll be *mine* the cops will want to cut," Lance went on infuriatedly. "I don't stand a chance getting a spot on another sheet if I wanted to quit—which I don't. But you can take your Northwest Mounted Police angle and——"

Julie, passing, caroled, "Good morning, Mr. Mc-Cleary. Hide under the table."

Lance's mouth was still open. Carl shook his head. "So you were that crocked last night . . ."

Lance closed his mouth. "She's crazy."

"Oh, Mr. McCleary," mocked Carl.

Lance knew he shouldn't have come to work this morning. "That's got nothing to do with this. If you think I'm going to be the fall-guy for you and have—" He clapped his hand to his forehead. *"Hide under the table?* Holy smoke!"

"What's the matter?"

Lance grinned, his wrath forgotten. " 'You made me what I am today, I hope you're satisfied.' "

Carl was mystified. "What were you drinking last night?"

"Brainstorms. You know what Julie just did? She threw a lead into my lap. I forgot all about it."

"I suppose the killer's waiting for you under that table," said Carl dryly.

"Or his friend," said Lance.

He started away and walked into two grim officers. "Who's McCleary here?" asked one of them.

The tone was a familiar one to Lance. Trouble. *What did I do last night?*

Carl rose, enjoying the intrusion. "You mean Lancelot Seumas McCleary?" he asked.

A couple of copy boys stared at the officers, pop-eyed. All over the room members of the staff were leaving their desks and converging to the spot.

"Yeah," said the cop. "Tall, skinny, redheaded reporter." He took in Lance's length with one slow deliberate look. "You're the bird."

They grabbed Lance under the arms, started out with him. "Hey, wait a minute, what's the charge?" he demanded.

"Don't try nothing funny," warned one of the cops, "or we'll have to get rough."

Dragged through the news room, Lance saw Carl laughing, Julie speechless, the staff surprisingly amused. He yelled, "Get a lawyer!"

Seventeen

Police Commissioner Blathmac Seanaman, short, swart and tousled, with a minimum of neck and a maximum of torso, took off his rumpled coat and leaned back in his big office chair with his feet dangling a foot from the floor, no picture of municipal dignity.

"McCleary," he snapped, "you've got a black heart."

"Me?" Lance was injured. "What about your strong-arm boys making that phony pinch?"

When the Commissioner flew off the handle, as he frequently did, his voice grew shrill. "I ordered you picked up soon as I read that headline. It's a cheap way to poke fun at the force."

"But I didn't have anything to do with it," protested Lance.

The Commissioner sprang up. Barrel-chested and haughty, he stamped about his swank office. "Don't give me that. What do you know about the killer that we don't?"

"Not a thing."

"What about that pawn ticket? How did you get it?"

"Through a fluke."

"That's fine," the Commissioner said sarcastically. "That explains everything."

Lance explained about the ticket.

"Well, part of that's believable. But how do you know the killer of Lonely Heart's the same man who got Pop Farnsworth?"

"Hunch."

To his native Ireland the Commissioner owed his temper, to New York his livelihood, to crime his fame and, at the moment, to Lance his apoplexy. "Quit playing Nick Carter! What are the facts?"

"Oh, facts. In the first place, Pop didn't phone my paper."

"Pipe-dream?"

Lance nodded. "And I didn't go to the hockshop. Julie Allison did."

"In other words you don't know a thing."

"That's what I said."

"And you're working on a hunch that Farnsworth knew too much and was killed by the Lonely Heart slayer."

"Right."

The phone rang. The Commissioner barked into it, "I told you to tell that ink-stained parasite not to bother me." He hung up. "Your boss. He's been calling me ever since you were picked up."

Lance grinned. "He's really a great guy when you get to know him."

"He's a menace, and so are you and so is that paper you work for. We've been at it day and night trying to track down that woman's identity. Next thing, Pop Farnsworth's killed and now we have two on the same card. Those stunts your boss pulls are going to get him into a mess one of these days."

"You've got to admit that so far he's ringing the bell."

"It's cheap. Papers today aren't what they used to be. They're trouble-makers, liars. Another thing— what's this about a killer hiding under the table?"

Lance said, "I give up. This is like a hick town. One crack and in ten minutes everybody knows it."

"Well, what about it?"

Lance shrugged. "Just a gag. Can I go now?"

The Commissioner was reluctant. "All right. But if I read about any arrests in your paper before we make them—"

"I'll tip you off first," said Lance. "How about a ride?"

The Commissioner snorted, but arranged for a police car to drive Lance anywhere he ordered. "If you make a slip," he said, "and happen to get your boss instead of the killer, I'll make you a lieutenant."

Lance had himself driven to the Park Row Café. Old Man Sweeney was grinding coffee in the kitchen, and in rhythm chewing tobacco and singing *Yankee Doodle* in a cracked quavering falsetto.

"Good morning, Lancelot."

"Johnny," said Lance, "tell Greeley to move over." Sweeney blinked, thought, got it. "Trouble?"

"Plenty."

The old man rubbed his hands excitedly. "Need help, eh?"

"That's what I'm here for."

"And I'm your man." Sweeney led the way to the same corner table. "Fire away, son."

Lance fired away. Sweeney listened intently.

"So now you want to know who saw him?" he said. "Well, you've come to the right place. Get back about —make it three. I'll have 'em all here by then."

Outside the café, Lance ruminated. He ought to go back to the office. But Carl had laughed when the cops hauled him out. Let Carl wait and worry.

Carl's angle had been that the killer hung around the pawnshop, wary, until Pop had happened by. The first logical step, then, was the shop.

He found the proprietor in great distress. The police had been there; they had questioned him; they had taken the ticket. Lance reflected amusedly that the Commissioner had wasted no time.

"And now they're sending detectives," moaned the dumpy little man. "You police—you're so bad for my business."

Lance allowed the impression that he was a plain-clothes man to remain.

"You knew Pop, didn't you?" he asked.

The proprietor brushed his face with his hands as if he had walked through cobwebs. "I'll tell you what I told them, Mr. McCleary. I'm an intellectual, an idealist. I ignore the flotsam and jetsam which floats past my store. But Pop—who didn't know him?"

He shook his head. "It's a disgrace to the newspaper profession to let a man like that be buried in Potter's Field."

Lance liked him for that. "He's being taken care of. Did you see him yesterday?"

"They asked that, too. Sure, I saw him. When didn't I see him?"

"I mean did he come in?"

"Why should he come in? Look, he was standing there." The proprietor's pointing finger placed Pop just outside the door.

"About when was this?"

"Right after I sold a camera. One of those old Univexes. That flapjack girl in Childs', she wanted it for months and yesterday she came in and bought it."

"What time was it?"

"Oh—the time. Why didn't you say so? It was about one. She told me she had to be back at her window grill by one and she was late."

About one . . . Lance made a mental note to remember that. "What was he doing—just standing there? Did he say anything?"

"He didn't say nothing to *me*."

Patience, McCleary, patience. "You mean he did speak to someone?"

"Oh, sure. The man who was standing there first. Pop came up and slapped him on the back and then—"

The man who was standing there first. "Wait a minute, about this man—who was he?"

"I should know? He was some fellow. He came

along and looked in my window display. He was a funny fellow."

"Funny?"

"You know what I mean—maybe he was embarrassed. In this business, Mr. McCleary, you know how it is, sometimes if it's the first time, it isn't easy to come in. I could tell you—"

"Some other time. But about this man—"

"Well, he went by once and then he came back and he stood there like he couldn't make up his mind and then Pop came up to him—and later he came back again and *still* he didn't come in."

Lance was tingling. But it had come too fast. "One thing at a time, please. Let's get this straight. This man went past once—right?"

"That's right."

That's how Carl had figured it. The killer was afraid to walk straight in with the ticket. "Then he came back."

"I told you."

He hung around trying to figure out a way. And then Pop— "And then Pop came along. You say he slapped the man on the back." *Then Pop must have known him.* "Then what happened?"

"What should happen? Pop touched him."

"For how much?"

"You think I got eyes like opera glasses?"

"But you're sure he got a handout? Could you hear what Pop said?"

"With my door closed? I don't listen to other people's conversation, Mr. McCleary. The man gave Pop something."

You're getting warmer and warmer. "What?"

"How should I know? He gave him something."

The ticket—he gave him the ticket. "Then what?"

"He went away like I told you."

"But Pop didn't come in."

"Look, Mr. McCleary, I already said he didn't."

It was all working out. "Which way did the man go?"

"That way."

That would be toward Hester Street. Before Lance could ask his next question, it was anticipated.

"Pop went that way too," said the proprietor.

That was odd. If Pop wanted to get away . . . But it didn't matter. "Then you say the man came back. Was he alone?"

"Yes."

"What did he do?"

"Nothing. He didn't stay long. Then he went away again and he never came back. Funny, no?"

He was waiting for Pop. But Pop had disappeared. "What did the man look like?"

"Like a man."

With an effort Lance kept his voice jocular. "Oh, come now. You must have some idea of his appearance."

The proprietor flashed a gold-toothed smile meant to be ingratiating. "I'm not a smart detective like you, Mr. McCleary."

"But was he short? Tall? Skinny? Fat? Did he wear a hat? What was he dressed like? Did you—"

"Wait, wait, Mr. McCleary. Let me show you. Here, come behind the counter." He waited until

Lance stood beside him. "Now," said the proprietor, "*you* look."

Lance watched the street. Men shuffled past the doorway; others idled to stare at the collection of junk in the window. One man loitered near the doorway for a few seconds, went on his way. Two girls stopped, one of them pointed at some article near the cameras. They left.

"Well?" asked the proprietor. "What did the third man look like?"

Even prepared as he had been, Lance couldn't remember. "You win," he said. He went to the door. "Thanks. That's all now."

"But tell me, Mr. McCleary, what is with this man —how he looked, where he went? I thought it was *Pop*."

"He may be the murderer."

"*Hah?*"

Lance closed the door behind him, looked back and grinned. The pawnbroker was still gaping at him. Lance waved and started in the direction of Hester Street.

Next door was a low vaudeville house. The girl in the booth said, "Oh, Pop Farnsworth. Isn't that a shame? I just read about him in the paper." But she didn't remember seeing him pass the day before.

He went on to a "haberdashery and firemen's outfits" and drew a blank there; to a notions shop which outfitted street merchants, hawkers, Times Square pitchmen, where the counter was cluttered with trick key rings, watches, fake matches, exploding cigars. The worn-out blonde behind it concentrated, vaguely

recollected Pop passing the store, but she wasn't posi-
tive—he had passed so often.

Lance continued with the frail, wistful meerschaum
carver next door. Surrounded by pipes he had made,
still exhibiting the gold medal his father had won at
the Philadelphia Centennial Exposition in 1876, the
small man was sorry he couldn't help; he had been
busy on a new pipe.

Lance didn't give up. He quizzed the cabinet-
maker, the pharmacist, the hardware dealer, the ham-
burger-stand owner, the gypsy fortune teller, the
round-shouldered owner of a second-hand clothing
store.

"Sure," said the clothes-dealer, "I saw him yesterday . . . right after I got through eatin'."

Lance took a deep breath. At last. "Was he alone?"

"No, he was followin' some guy. Pop was puttin'
the bee on him."

"How far did he follow him?"

"I could only see to the corner. I was outside takin'
it easy. I got a kick out the way Pop was makin' this
guy nervous. I could tell."

So the killer had been nervous. Lance didn't doubt
it. "Which way did they go then?"

"The guy beat it fast around the corner."

"Toward Chrystie?"

"Yeah—and then Pop went high-tailin' after him."

"What did this man look like?"

"Search me."

"You mean you can't even remember whether he
was tall or—"

The clothes-dealer shrugged. "Who cares? I seen

Pop milk so many guys I don't pay no attention to the sucker."

"You didn't hear what they said, did you?"

"Too far away."

"Thanks."

"There's somethin' else, mister."

Lance turned back quickly. The clothes-dealer beckoned with both hands. "For eighteen-fifty I got a blue pin-stripe just your size. It'll bring you luck."

Lance escaped the clutching hands just in time. He went around the corner. There was Chrystie and beyond that Forsyth and Eldridge and Allen and Orchard . . . Pop could have gone to one of a dozen places on each street. Lance dropped into a few saloons, learned Pop hadn't been at any of the local bars the day before.

He recalled that it had been early in the afternoon when Pop had wheedled the eight dollars out of him. He wondered if Pop had said anything to Julie about the ticket other than what he, Lance, had heard. It would be a good idea to make the *Comet* his next step.

The Wall Street Close edition was out; he glanced at the headline: COMET REPORTER ARRESTED. The subhead was even better: MCCLEARY GRILLED— "KNOWS TOO MUCH!" POLICE RESENT REFUSAL TO BARE VITAL FACTS.

Lance couldn't help chuckling. Blathmac would rave when he read that. That crazy Carl; he'd headline a grunt if it had anything to do with the story.

The boy at the information desk leaped up as Lance

came out of the elevator. "Gee, Mr. McCleary, what'd they do? They grill you? Third degree?"

"They were pretty tough," said Lance seriously.

He went on to Julie's office. Excited and indignant at the same time, she was all questions and exclamations.

"Don't believe what you read in your own paper," he told her.

He made her go over every word Pop had said, but learned nothing.

Carl was waiting for him.

"Why didn't you phone? What happened?"

Lance rolled his eyes.

"They should've thrown you into solitary!" snorted Carl. "What've you been doing?"

"Getting 'vital facts,'" said Lance.

"Give me *one*."

"Pop knew the killer."

That was vital enough Lance could see. Carl said slowly. "Who told you that?"

Lance gave him a rapid digest of his conversation with the pawnbroker.

"Could he describe the man?" asked Carl.

"None of them could."

"What do you mean none of them?"

Lance recounted his coverage of the block. He saw grudging admiration in Carl's look and affected nonchalance. "See you later."

"Where you going now?" said Carl.

"I'm not finished collecting vital facts. Got a hunch one of 'em will lead me straight to the killer."

"Don't forget to let me in on it," drawled Carl.

Eighteen

Lance found the Park Row Café transformed into the meeting room of a rescue mission. It smelled of old fish, filth, sour milk and sweat. Some twenty bums were crowding the place. Lance, taller than any of them, could see Sweeney holding forth in the rear—he was telling three of them they were welcome to the washroom but he'd crack the head of the first one who dirtied it.

He saw Lance. "Come on in, boy."

All faces turned to Lance. His eyes swept over them. This was the circle of human scum in which Pop had moved—these derelicts, corner cripples, lushers, tipsters, slophouse stock. Feeling like a plutocrat, he pushed through aging failure to Sweeney.

"Told you my grapevine would work," said the old man triumphantly. "Every one of 'em seen Pop yesterday."

"I've got to hand it to you. How'd you do it?"

"Passed the word there'd be no more grub handouts unless," said Sweeney simply. "Now go ahead an' start your spiel. An' don't let 'em scare you, I'm right behind you." He raised his voice, addressing them, "This here's my friend, Lancelot McCleary of the *Comet*—"

"The *Times* keeps you warmer," said a bum.

There was a ripple of laughter. Sweeney glared. "He's tryin' to get some idea together to help him find the man who killed Pop—"

"How about some grub first?" shouted a one-eyed souse.

A chorus followed his demand. Sweeney's eyes blazed. He whipped a cane from the hands of a seated cripple and brandished it angrily. "Listen, y'dirty bums!" he shouted. "I've never turned one of you away an' you know it. How many cups o' coffee, bowls of mush an' hunks o' meat have I dished out to you? Now you dish out to me, y'hear? No talk—no grub."

Lance was sorry for them; their eyes darted from the enraged Sweeney to the pies on the shelf, the steaming soup and beef-stew pots.

Still breathing fire Sweeney turned to him. "Now go on, Lancelot. First one gives you trouble I'll crack his head."

Lance cleared his throat, not knowing how to begin. They were staring at his shoes, his nails, his tie, staring blankly, apathetically. He cleared his throat again. "Men," he began, knowing instantly it was a hollow and pale opening, "what happened to Pop Farnsworth could have happened to any one of you."

It didn't seem to matter to any of them.

"The killer is still at large. Understand?" he went on as if he were addressing a group of ten-year-olds. "The man who killed Pop is still walking around. He might pick out one of you. How would you like to have your head bashed in like Pop?"

The only head-bashing they seemed interested in was Sweeney's cane.

"Sweeney tells me you saw Pop yesterday. I want to know everything. When you saw him, where, was he with anyone, did he say anything, was he drunk, was he sober—anything and everything I can think of —I'll ask. Now, are you men ready?"

Silence.

Sweeney lifted the cane. They rose and roared proof that they were ready. Close-mouthed moochers became loquacious; gabble spread through the café; mutes were suddenly long-winded. Lance had to shout for order.

"One at a time," he cried. "You—" he pointed to a pot-bellied bum. "Where did you see Pop?"

"At Cherry and Market."

"About what time?"

The bum sucked false teeth in. "Mm—'bout five I guess. They was listenin' to the radio."

"What radio?"

"There's only one there."

"Where?"

"At the Shamrock."

"Did Pop stay there long?"

"He was there when I came in."

"What time was that?"

"I just told you. Five o'clock."

"How long did he stay there?"

"He didn't. He was raisin' hell with the radio when

I went in. You know Pop, he didn't like swing music."

"So you're sure he left the Shamrock about five?"

"Yeah."

"How drunk was he?"

"Stiff—an' flashin' a roll."

"He didn't flash no roll when I seen him," said a hollow-cheeked sickly tramp.

Lance turned to him. "When was that?"

"Can't remember. Say about two. Maybe a little later."

"Where?"

"James Street."

"What direction was he coming from?"

"New Bowery."

"Tell you where he was going?"

"Nope, but he didn't flash no roll. I know Pop. If he had a roll he'd a'flashed it."

Lance shot questions at the others. Some of them had seen Pop near Hester. What time? About one or thereabouts. Alone? Yes, he was alone. Others remembered running into him on Chatham Square. What time? Oh, a little after one.

"How 'bout that grub?" cackled the one-eyed souse.

"Shut up!" blared Sweeney.

"But I seen Pop," whined the one-eyed souse.

"When?" asked Lance.

"This mornin'."

"Throw him out!" roared the bums.

The one-eyed souse was given the bum's rush. Sweeney waved the cane. "Any more wise guys?"

A horny bum said, "I seen Pop last night."

"Where?"

"Keene's."

"What time?"

"Lemme see . . . I hadda leave to get to th' mission's second feedin'. Y'know, son, once y'miss that feed bag y'got one more chance, but when y'miss that second chance, y'don't get even a whiff of them pork chops or pigs' feet or—"

"What time?"

"Seven on th' nose."

"Was he alone?"

"Sure."

"Still flashing a roll?"

"Nope."

"Did you leave before he did?"

"Nope, right after him."

"And you saw him walking off?"

"Sure, they was gonna kill th' bottle. Pop gimme a swig of it. Bonded stuff. He must've scratched a sucker an'—"

Lance dodged through tables and leaped upon the startled man. "You said *they* were going to kill the bottle!"

The man found his tongue. "Yeah."

"I thought you said he was alone?"

"In Keene's he was. I meant outside—"

"In other words you saw him leave Keene's seven o'clock last night—alone—and outside the joint he met a man. That right?"

"Yeah."

"The man was waiting for him?"

"Dunno . . . Pop was cryin'."

"*Why?*"

"*I* dunno. Didn't say a word to me. I dropped into Keene's to use th' can an' on th' way out Pop gimme a swig an' I beat it to th' mission."

"And you saw him walk off with that stranger?"

"Yeah."

"Tall man?"

"Dunno."

"Short man?"

"Dunno."

"Well, was he fat or skinny or a cripple or did he wear glasses or a beard or a hat?"

"Dunno."

"Was he a bum?"

"Dunno . . . I had no time to see. I hadda beat it back to Chatham Square."

"Which way did they go?"

"They headed for th' river."

"Did the stranger poke his head into Keene's?"

"Dunno."

"Pop just walked out, then, as if the stranger were waiting for him?"

"Yeah, I guess so. He walked out hangin' onto his bottle an' cryin'."

Lance felt his scalp creep. Why had Pop been crying? Had it been fear? Could it have been fear? Had he had an inkling of what was coming?

He faced the others. "Did anyone see him after seven o'clock last night?"

They pondered, disputed among themselves. Some of them enjoyed playing detective, others felt important; most of them didn't seem to give a damn. One pock-marked parasite rose.

"I was takin' a snooze on the *Journal* platform when he come out."

"From where?"

"Charlie's."

"What time?"

"Two o'clock."

"Oh."

The bum mistook Lance's disappointment, defended himself. "I know it was two 'cause the Salvation Army tries their high c's every day in front of Newsboys' Home at two. They woke me up."

"Did you speak to him?"

"Nope."

"Did anyone meet him?"

"I don't think so. He was alone when he came out an' I—"

"Did you go into Charlie's?"

"Nah. Pop's the only guy which ever got a shot on the house at Charlie's."

"Which way did he go?"

"Search me. I went back to sleep."

"Say, mister!" came a shout from the rear.

"Fire away, Grubby," encouraged Sweeney.

Grubby, an old-school hobo, shuffled to the front. "I remember meetin' Pop. It wasn't seven yet. He had a fistful of dough."

"Where was that?"

"Not far from my flop . . . 'round Cherry an' Oliver."

"Dip's?"

"He could'a'been headin' for Dip's. Yeah, come to think of it, he was goin' to Dip's."

Lance raised his voice. "Anyone see him at Dip's Tavern?"

A wrinkled midget, armless, stamped his feet on the floor. "Me!"

Lance lifted the midget to a table. "What time was that?"

"Around three. He asked Dip for a pint of Black Gold an' was thrown out. Then I seen him countin' paper money. So did Dip an' he got him back again. Pop told him to go to hell but Dip gave him a shot on the house an' Pop got his Black Gold. That's bonded stuff, y'know."

"Did anyone see him between five and seven?" asked Lance.

In a few minutes by a ferocious arithmetical dispute between them, he had one thing clarified: no one had seen Pop between five and seven or after he left Keene's.

He sorted out his information methodically. He had made no notes; they weren't necessary. His mind sifted, tabulated, filed. Now he could figure out where Pop went after he turned the corner at Bowery and Hester; according to the time, he had made his way directly down Chatham Square to Charlie's. Too many had seen him on the Square between one and one-fifteen, and it would only take about fifteen minutes to get to Charlie's from the pawnshop.

From Charlie's Pop had gone to the *Comet;* he himself had seen him about two-fifteen in Julie's office, perhaps two-thirty.

The midget had seen him at Dip's around three;

the pot-bellied bum vouched it was five when Pop was at the Shamrock.

It wasn't so complicated now: Pop left the *Comet* a capitalist with eight dollars and dropped into Dip's, just a couple blocks away, got his pint of Black Gold, hung around for drinks, then went to the Shamrock. If he left the Shamrock at five and Keene's at seven, where was he between those hours? He may have contacted the killer, arranged to meet him at Keene's by seven. He had been crying. It was just possible he made that seven o'clock appointment with the killer.

"Do yourself any good?" asked Sweeney.

"Can't tell yet."

Sweeney bristled. "If you think they're holdin' out on you—"

Lance laughed. "No, they came through. Put the feed bag on them and I'll get a fat check for you from the paper."

Sweeney frowned. "I ain't doin' this for the paper. I'm doin' it for you, son."

Lance patted him on the back. "I know, Johnny— and thanks. But what the hell, it's not out of my pocket."

Following the route he had been able to map out as having been taken by Pop the day before, Lance went first to Charlie's.

The fat bartender was unashamedly emotional.

"There'll never be another Mr. Farnsworth," he sighed.

But he was unable to help Lance. Pop had paid

for and downed ten drinks, sung songs and seemed happy. That was all Charlie knew.

"You're sure he didn't say anything about a pawn ticket?" asked Lance.

"Not a word."

"He didn't happen to mention where he got the dollar?"

"No, but he told me he'd be back with more money —lots of it, he said."

Lance mulled that over. Pop had had only the one dollar at that time. Had the killer given it to him to go into the pawnshop and find out what had been pawned and what it would cost to redeem it? Or had it been a much larger sum which Pop had squandered quickly? But what made him so sure he was going to get more money? Would it have been from the killer—or had Pop known then that he was going to tap Julie? It was a problem for which Lance could find no answer. He was confident that he would.

Pop had spent an hour or so at Charlie's; according to the itinerary he had gone from there to the *Comet*. Lance skipped that, went directly to Dip's Tavern.

He learned that Pop had breezed in about a quarter to three, had left forty-five minutes later; it was at Dip's that the first of the embezzled eight dollars had been flourished and spent. But that was all; no one could remember anything Pop had said.

The next stop was the Shamrock . . . Pop had stumbled in about three-forty-five, remained until five.

"Any idea where he went from here?" asked Lance.

The bull-necked bartender tugged at his ear,

squinted, had no idea about anything. But an ancient Negro shining the footrail looked up and said softly, "I know. Pop told me. He was my friend. I hope you get the man who killed him, mister."

There was something about the sad, doggy eyes that got Lance. He said, "He was my friend too. That's why I'm trying to— Where'd he go?"

"To Sal's."

Would this fill the gap between five and seven in Pop's route? Lance hurried to Water and Market Streets and entered Tammany Sal's broken-down bar. She was alone. Sprawled at a table, she was reading a love story magazine. Her body sagged with memories, but her face had a personality undisturbed by days of neglect. It was beautiful. Sloppy, dirty, her body was a nightmare, her face a voluptuary's dream. Looking at it, he could believe the stories about her and the prominent men who had loved her. She had out-beautied all the Bowery hetaerae and achieved her name through being the political bigwigs' robust delight.

When he ran copy she had loved to tease him about his innocence; and once when he delivered a message to his editor, she had kissed him. He could still remember his blush.

"Hello, Sal."

She lifted her eyes. "Who're you?"

"Don't remember me, do you?" She was looking at him steadily. "I'm Lance McCleary. I used to—"

"That redheaded kid!" She got to her feet, put her hands on his arms. "My God, you're big—a real skyscraper. Here, sit down."

She pushed him into a chair, stood over him. "All grown-up now, aren't you, kid? But that carrot brillo is still the same." She ran her fingers through his hair. "Red and thick and—hot . . ."

He was embarrassed. He was twenty-eight and a top crime reporter, he had seen mayhem, rape, corruption—but he was embarrassed. He ducked his head as if he were the copy boy again. She laughed and sat down opposite him.

"What can I do for you, boy—I hope?"

"It's about Pop Farnsworth."

She groaned. "Ah, poor old Richard. Too bad . . . and here I was drinking with him just last night."

"What time was that?"

"After five sometime."

"How long was he here, Sal?"

"Left after six. Say, you got nice eyes."

"Thanks. How was he?"

"Like a board," she said. "I've seen him stiff, but last night—" she whistled.

"No, I mean did he act as if he was afraid of something—someone?"

"Not Richard. You know, Red, you got nice hands too."

"Ah, come on Sal, this is serious."

Her leg pressed against his. "So am I."

"Look, all I'm trying to find out is whether he said something—anything that might give me a lead on who killed him."

"You're wasting your time. He was probably rolled. How old are you now?"

"Did he say anything about a ticket?"

Her eyes were laughing. "Old enough to know now, aren't you?"

"Try to remember, Sal," begged Lance.

"I will if you hold my hand."

He held her hand. She squeezed his. She said, "He *did* say something about a ticket . . ."

He was suspicious. "What kind?"

"Hockshop."

He leaned forward. "What did he say?"

She glanced around. "It's not comfortable here, Red. Let's go upstairs to my—"

He caught himself stammering. "Sorry, Sal, I'm on the job now."

"You mean maybe later—?"

"Maybe," he lied.

She released his hand, threw back her head and roared with laughter. "All right, Red, I won't kid you anymore . . . I don't know what he said. He was so drunk I couldn't make out anything; probably didn't know what he was talking about himself."

"Is that all?"

"Sorry, honey. Oh—he broke half-a-buck for some nickels."

"What for?"

"He wanted to make a call, he said."

"*To whom?*"

"I haven't got a phone here." She sighed. "It isn't like it used to be. They all used to come to see Tammany Sal. Now I haven't even got a phone."

"But didn't he mention whom he wanted to call?"

"No."

He rose. "Well, thanks, Sal."

"It's all right, Red." She walked him to the door. "You still got nice eyes." She laughed again and patted his backside as he left.

He walked to Keene's slowly. So Pop had wanted to make a call . . . Had he made it? And from where?

Keene was a treasure-store of Bowery biography. He had reached the sentimental sixties and was infatuated with his own reminiscences. But for once he forgot them when Lance mentioned Pop.

"They get the fella yet?" he asked.

"Cops are still looking for him."

"You got an idea?"

"Digging for one. He left here seven last night, didn't he?"

"Uh-huh."

"What time did he get here?"

"Little after six. He was over at Sal's."

Lance took a chance. "Did he make a call from here?"

"Yeah—from the booth."

Lance's nerves tightened. "Did you hear him?"

"No, he shut the door. Said he was going to call some chap, said he had to."

"How long was he on the phone?"

"About a minute or two."

"What time was that?"

"A little before seven. Maybe a quarter to—maybe six-thirty."

"What did he do then?"

"Came back to the bar and stood here drinking and crying into his whisky."

There it was again—crying . . . "Was he crying *before* or *after* he came out of the booth?"

"After. He came out blubbering like a kid."

Lance almost slammed his fist down on the bar. He *had* been right. Pop had known the killer, had called to make an appointment to meet him, the killer had probably threatened him over the phone and Pop had wept because he was scared . . . "Did he watch that clock as if he had a date?" he asked.

Keene was getting bored with the subject. "Look, McCleary—Pop wasn't the only customer. You know, you remind me—"

He was getting ready to dip into history. Lance said quickly, "Didn't he make any crack about having to meet somebody?"

"No. As I was saying—"

"Did you see anyone waiting for him outside?"

"No." Keene gave up Lance as a listener. "Here." He shoved a bottle and a glass at Lance and went around the bar to a customer at a table. His voice came back, raised in loving recital.

Lance absently poured himself a drink, but with the glass an inch from his lips thought better of it. Not after last night. He put it down and leaned on the bar. Now what? He had interviewed a great many people, had covered a lot of territory; he had enough leads for dozens of short stories, boxed human interest profiles, unusual quotes, unusual backgrounds, unusual characters. But he had no lead on the killer. He was right back where he had started from.

Yet he knew he was close to something—he sensed it. All this groping . . .

"Are you McCleary?"

He turned from the bar. A miserable specimen of a man, filthy and furtive, waited for his answer.

"Yes."

Large unusually lucid and brilliant eyes met his. "You don't know me, do you?"

"No."

"I'm not a man," whispered the stranger. "I'm fifty-five years old, have four human children, six human grandchildren, weigh about one hundred and forty pounds; I eat, sleep, scratch myself and hate lice; but I am not a man."

He came closer. "I'm a lot of things, McCleary. I'm the black sheep of Gotham's flock, the whisky breath of Stephen Foster, the oldest street in the United States, the tea-water pump. I am the Henry Astor of the Fly Market, Priest of the Parish, Murderer's Alley, the Dead Rabbits. I am exaggerated humor, intense filth. I am an accomplished linguist, can hold my tongue in English, Spanish, French, Italian, German, Hungarian, Polish, Yiddish. I am the rise of the gangs. I am also a mystery. I am Bowery."

There was an explanation for the eyes and all this. "You're full of hop," said Lance.

"Yes-s," hissed the stranger.

"Well, what do you want?"

"Nothing." A bony finger was pointed at Lance. "It's you. You want something."

"Such as?"

"Information. I have it."

"About Pop?" Lance was skeptical.

"I can help you, McCleary."

"What do you know?"

"Nothing. But a friend of mine saw Pop yesterday; his account of Farnsworth's doings, I assure you, will interest you."

"Where is this friend?"

The stranger put his head to one side. "High stakes make the turn of the wheel interesting."

What could he lose? "Five bucks if he knows anything," said Lance.

"The game has begun." The stranger put out his hand. "At least a dollar for the first turn. A mere formality."

Lance gave it to him. "Let's go."

The hophead lagged behind. "Oh," said Lance. "Just a fake, eh?"

"Not at all. Do not misinterpret my hesitation."

Lance lost his temper. "Quit stalling for another touch! Get going or I'll have Sweeney put the finger on you."

It worked. "Come," said the hophead. "I shall lead the way . . ."

The Elite Hotel on Bowery near Pump Street was flanked by wretched store fronts. Lance followed him up the stairs and past the clerk's cage on the first landing, with its variety of signs: No Credit; No Fighting; No Spitting. The place stank of disinfectants.

A score of bums were in a big room, most of them asleep on iron cots. There was a triple row of these coffin-bunks, narrow lockers between them, and hanging overhead were unshaded electric bulbs encased in metal mesh. The hophead went down the second row and halted in front of a cot. Lance, right behind him, saw a bulky bum hugging the dirty sheet, snoring loudly. He smelled of disinfectant, stale meat and sweat collected between rolls of fat.

"This is he," said the hophead.

Lance shook a blubbery shoulder roughly. The fat man snorted. "I paid my dime."

"Get up," snapped Lance. Merciless, he wouldn't allow the leviathan to drop back to sleep. Eyes still closed, the bum heaved himself up, swung his feet to the floor. Lance fired a question at him.

The fat man wiped his face with his sleeve. "Sure I seen 'im," he mumbled. "Right near th' hockshop."

"Alone?"

"No. He was— Hey, who're you?"

"Never mind me. If you saw him with the right guy you'll make yourself twenty bucks."

The fat man, wide awake, got to his feet. "Whaddya wanna know?"

"When did you see Pop?"

" 'Bout one."

The hophead jabbed a finger into the belly that gave. "Go on," he commanded, "tell McCleary what you told us today."

"All I told 'em was I seen Pop workin' a sucker an' I yelled him good luck," said the fat man plaintively.

"Do you remember the sucker?"

"Sure."

It couldn't be true. "You mean you know what he looks like?"

"Sure."

Lance's voice rose. "You can identify him?"

"Sure."

"Don't talk! Don't say another word! *Come on.*"

Lance grabbed him. Let him stink. He was precious.

Nineteen

Carl saw a palpably excited Lance dragging a fat bum by one arm through the city room. The bum seemed bewildered, breathless; he was flapping one hand as if to give himself air . . . He watched their progress amusedly. Was this Lance's ultimate "vital fact?"

Then suddenly the air was alive with danger. A bum . . . *The Bowery*. He saw me—I know it! I was a fool. I should never have gone down. No—I wouldn't have been noticed if it hadn't been for *Pop* . . .

Not until they reached him did Lance release the bum; he swung him around to the side of the desk. Lance was red-faced, panting. "I've got the man who can identify the killer."

I knew he would say that. Now this bum will point at me and yell, "That's him!"

The fat man came closer, bent toward him. Carl drew back from the stench that came to him in a wave.

"*You* th' boss?"

Does that surprise him? His kind instinctively

respects authority. Maybe that will make him unsure . . .

"I told him I'd take him right to the boss himself," explained Lance.

The bum must have described the man. Lance couldn't have connected the description with me. How could he? There's nothing unusual about me. The bum's hesitating. I was right. He's afraid. He *is* unsure. He's nobody and I . . . "Well, come on, don't waste my time. You saw the killer?"

"Yessir."

"Where?"

"I seen him with Pop near Brown's hockshop."

He's staring at me. He's thinking he must have made a mistake, it couldn't be *me* he saw, not the boss. "You can describe him?"

"Yessir."

I mustn't be too impatient. It might make him truculent. Then he'll *want* to accuse me. "Go ahead. What does he look like?"

Lance took a cigarette from a pack. The bum gestured for one. Lance gave it to him. The bum waited for a light. Lance struck a match. The bum took a long puff.

His manner's changed; making Lance light the cigarette for him has given him assurance.

"Stand up, willya?" said the fat man.

Not that tone to me, you bum!

"Will ya stand up, please?" said the fat man.

I've got to get up . . . Lance looks surprised. He hadn't expected this. And afterward I mustn't be excited or angry. I must act as if I thought the bum was drunk and tell Lance to throw him out. But I mustn't overdo it, I mustn't talk too much. I must make Lance forget it.

He rose. The fat man studied him, enjoying momentary importance, taking his time.

What is he waiting for? Why doesn't he say it?

"Yeah, that's what I figgered," said the bum. "He was 'bout th' same size as you."

And?

" 'Bout as old as you too, I guess."

And?

"He wasn't wearin' no topcoat."

And?

The bum was looking at him as if he expected comment. Was he finished? Could that be all? "What else?"

"Nothin'."

"You mean that's all?"

"Gee, mister, it wasn't *me* puttin' th' bee on 'm."

He doesn't recognize me, he doesn't remember me, he didn't from the beginning! Or is he cleverer than I thought? Is he waiting to shake me down later? No, poor bastard, he's being honest about this in his own stupid way.

He turned to Lance. "So you've got the man . . ."

Lance was dismayed. "I thought . . . I wouldn't let him talk. I wanted you to get it fresh."

Carl sat down. It was good to sit down, good not to have to watch himself any more. He asked the bum crisply, "Didn't he have any distinguishing features? A beard? Glasses? Did he limp? Was he doing anything with his hands? Did you notice anything about his voice?"

"He wasn't talkin'," said the fat man sullenly.

"That's no description. It could fit any man. It could fit me."

The fat man squirmed. "Down goes McCleary," said Lance.

"Want to make ten dollars?" asked Carl.

The bum hiked up his pants. "*He* said it'd be twenny."

"He's a philanthropist," said Carl dryly. "But all right. Can you write your name?"

"Sure." The bum was proud. He scrawled it across a sheet of copy paper.

Carl gave the autograph to a passing boy. "Get a one-column cut on this." He phoned the cashier. "I'm signing a voucher for twenty dollars to Ben Bailey. Honor it." He handed it to the bum. "You'll get your money from the cashier. Upstairs, one flight. Thanks. Sign this release, too."

"Tell you one thing, Mr. Chapman," said the bum humbly. "Next time I see that guy, I'll know 'm."

"Good. You can go now."

"How 'bout another cigarette?" Lance gave him the near-emptied pack. Clutching it and the voucher as if they were equally rare, the bum lumbered off.

Lance hunched his shoulders and jammed his hands into his pockets. "Go on, say it."

"Forget it," said Carl. "You know what to do. His signature will make a good byline. Put it in Bowery lingo. The police will have him identifying every picture in their files."

"I must have been tired. He was last on the list."

"What list?"

Lance was disgusted. "I know every dive Pop was in from the time he left the hockshop until he was killed."

"How'd you find that out?"

"Here." Lance pulled a folded sheet of paper from his pocket, tossed it across the desk.

Carl opened it. It was a crudely sketched diagram with lines drawn, names and figures printed inexpertly; it was dotted with crosses and circles. "What's this?"

"Map. Eight bucks carried him a long way. I had to draw that to figure things out. Those're the names of saloons. Even marked the time he got to each one and the time he left."

"So that's what you were doing this afternoon."

Beginning with Sweeney's bums, Lance went through his expedition. Carl kept his face blank. He respected Lance's thoroughness, but he knew Lance felt no admiration for himself, expected none from him.

"But after Keene's—blank," said Lance.

"So Pop really did phone someone."

"Yep. Got to hand it to you, Carl. You certainly called the shot. Only thing you left out was that Pop knew the killer. . . . Want an eye-witness slant, huh?"

" 'I Saw the Killer, by Ben Bailey.' "

Lance grunted, returned to his desk. Carl snapped the creases from the map. He could use it. But Lance must be stopped.

From now on I must know every move he makes. That was my mistake, letting him dig on his own. No more of that.

From now on Lance's energy must be replaced by indifference, his tenacity by boredom. He was the editor, Lance the reporter. The slayer of Lonely Heart would never be found, but the search would go on—and the editor would direct it. Let Lance be the avenger. The editor would throw him tips—and dissipate them; create leads—and squash them. Let Lance be relentless. Let him dig up clue after clue—and bring them in to the editor who planted them. Lance was his only danger. But there was a weapon against that danger. Carl leaned back. When I get through with him, he'll be begging to forget a story he should never have broken.

Twenty

For six consecutive days now the front page of the *Comet* had been the most sensational lighthouse in U.S. journalism. The *Comet* was the paper-of-the-week. Lonely Heart had caught on.

In a drawer of Carl's desk was a copy of Editor & Publisher. ". . . Only where the banner of a free press still flaps could such a journalistic phenomenon as Carl Chapman continue to exist. He could put a paper together with a pair of scissors and a footrule and still nurse it into the best-paying, hardest-hitting publication on the Atlantic seaboard."

Three days ago he had started the first of the Bible quotations—boxed in the lower right-hand corner of page one—a sixteen-inch red arrow pointing downward to it:

> *Leaving his death for an example of a noble courage, and a memorial of virtue, not only unto young men, but unto all his nations.*
>
> *Maccabees.VI,31.*

That had been for Lance's obituary of Pop Farnsworth—the sloppiest writing job that had ever crossed

Carl's desk. But he had it set up, word for word, tear for tear, and planted it smack under the bannerline, between a two-column of Pop in his heyday on the old *Globe,* another of Pop's ultimate worldly belongings: a fedora, a meal ticket, two dollars and twenty-eight cents.

Madison had bleated, "Sacreligious!"

But Carl had followed it with Ben Bailey's ghosted eye-witness story, and:

> *A faithful witness will not lie: but a deceitful witness uttereth a lie.*
> *The Book of Proverbs.XIV,5.*

Now the Street Final carried the third arrow shooting down across a shrewdly salvaged account of Lance's appeal to Sweeney, the Bowery grapevine, the bums, to:

> *Faithful are the wounds of a friend.*
> *The Book of Proverbs.XXVII,5.*

Lance's map was blown up to three columns.

But there was also a center-boxed announcement. Carl chuckled. Madison must have received a copy the same time he had. At any minute, the publisher would send for him.

Instead, Madison appeared in person. The splutter of typewriters increased. "Mr. Chapman!" he bawled and stormed back to his office. Carl followed. He knew what to expect.

"I've just seen the Street Final," snapped Madison.

"I must insist that before you gamble with my money, you inform me!"

If he only knew how safe his money is. "It's only ten thousand," said Carl.

"Only ten thousand?" Madison dropped into his chair. "First you offered five, now ten! Do you intend to increase the reward for the capture of the killer day by day?"

Carl noticed a new picture on the wall: Madison and a senator. "You have nothing to worry about. The reward will never be paid. There were more than twenty-five hundred unsolved murders last year. Next year Pop and Lonely Heart will be on this year's list."

"Hmph. Well . . ."

Now he's finished with that, thought Carl.

"One more thing . . ." Madison scratched the side of his nose nervously. "It seems your name came up this morning at the N.P.A." He fidgeted. "It was rather an unpleasant affair. They were profoundly skeptical of your tactics. They even went so far as to brand you" —he cleared his throat— "as a fraud, a promoter, an exploiter of the achievements of others."

"That so?"

Madison rose, bounced about the office with short rubbery steps. He stuttered on; the Newspaper Publishers Association had pointed out that the ethics of journalism were endangered by Carl Chapman's: irreverent, blatant, cynical.

Carl Chapman's . . . He loved every offense Madison chalked up against him in the report. He pictured them trying to buck his tide, damning his copy

as backhouse literature, his front page as a crusade
for crime.

"In fact," said Madison, "Mr. Jaediker said that
the *Comet,* under your whip, had no honest or con-
structive purpose!"

So Jaediker of the *Chronicle* had been in on the
kill. When Carl was rewrite on the *Chronicle* he had
envied Jaediker. Now . . . What other city editor
had ever been the target of denunciation by the dic-
tators of the press? He knew what rankled them. They
were rich, powerful, good businessmen with country-
club complexes, but bad newspapermen. Editors, to
them, never got rich; they got testimonials and
healthy abuse. But he was different. He was a good
editor and a good businessman. They would never
swallow that combination. Poor Madison—squirm-
ing, frightened, speechless, lacking courage to stump
for his own paper, editor or face.

"And what did you tell them you were going to do
about me and my whip?" said Carl lightly.

For the first time, Madison's chipmunk cheeks
moved to make room for a smile. "I believe they're all
envious."

Do tell. "You'd better stand by for another kaffee-
klatsch."

"What do you mean?"

"When they learn today's figure: seven-eighty-
three."

Madison was an inverted exclamation point.
"Seven hundred and eighty-three thousand . . ." he
said, awed.

"Net paid."

"Incredible."

"Just the beginning."

Madison paled. "Beginning?" he squeaked. "You mean you can't make that circulation hold?"

Carl smiled. "What's in it for me when I reach the miracle mark?"

Madison gulped. "Impossible."

Carl waited. Madison approached him on tiptoe. "Are you in earnest?"

"How much?"

"I'll give you"—Madison bit his lower lip—"ten thousand dollars." He pondered. Carl knew he was figuring, rapidly and raggedly as he could, the ABC rating; advertising that would double in linage and rates.

Carl thought of the fat bum. "Make it twenty thousand," he said, "and I'll peddle a million *Comets* for you—and sell them."

Madison took a deep breath. "All right, Chapman —it's a deal."

On his way out, Carl said, "Put it in writing."

In the city room he saw Lance at the typewriter roll in a book of copy paper and carbons, slug it violently and begin to write with a bitter expression on his face. Carl lit a cigar. He sent for the circulation chart and studied it carefully.

A book of copy was tossed on his desk. "Get someone else to finish this," said Lance.

Carl laughed. "Still burned up?"

"I was drunk, didn't know what I was writing. No guy in his right mind would have run that obit on Pop. It was high-school stuff and you know it."

"On the contrary." Carl enjoyed the vigorous rebellion. "You made every word carve its meaning deeply."

"Sure, sure, the laugh's on me. You had a swell time letting the whole world know McCleary's a sentimental windbag who weeps over copy in the backroom of a bar." He threw his hands out. "Why did you have to run it verbatim?"

A copy boy darted in front of him with a wire flash. "Here's something," said Carl after he read it. "UP just shot this tear-jerker on the shoe clerk." He shoved it into Lance's hand. "Here's your chance to redeem yourself. He has a battery of lawyers peddling alibis for him. They say he's insane; they're getting the press to play that up. You paint him sane. He raped a girl, killed her. He knew what he was doing and he's got to burn. Now quit sulking and burn him."

He relit his cigar. . . . If he could paralyze the *Eagle* he'd hijack that noon crowd in Brooklyn, an easy forty thousand. There were twenty thousand waiting for him in the Bronx if he could cripple the *Home News.* Why not a complete section for each borough—four pages? And across the Hudson—the *Journal* and *Hudson-Dispatch* would battle his invasion, but there were some thirty thousand Jerseyites who ate up Manhattan melodrama.

He phoned the president of the Lonely Hearts Club and made arrangements to open offices in the Bronx, Brooklyn, Richmond and Queens. He loved the challenge: one million roll.

"But you yourself said you had no obvious motives, Mr. McCleary," he heard Julie say.

Lance was leaning back in his chair, juggling coffee in a leaky container. "Got one now. Pop," he said.

"But he's not the key. Lonely Heart is. You told me—"

"Look, forget it, will you honey?"

"But it's beginning to show in your face. You're losing weight, Mr. McCleary. You can't afford to lose weight."

"Want me to throw the towel in, huh?"

She nodded.

"Nothing doing," he said. "I've got a personal interest that isn't going to be so easy to chill."

Carl nursed his ash. Lance, that's what you think. . . .

Twenty-One

Lance leaned back in his chair and stared moodily at a hostile typewriter. He felt a stranger at his own desk, an old and weary stranger, staggering under the biggest hoax in the *Comet's* life.

McCleary, you're ruined. At twenty-eight, you're ruined. A brilliant career as criminologist-reporter is being brought to a slow and ridiculous close. And all in a week's time.

And whose fault is it? Carl's—that's who. No, it isn't. Quit kidding yourself, McCleary. Sure, he made you the guinea pig. But can you blame him? Look what it did to circulation. It's your own fault. You had to be the hero, the golden boy. You had to say Lonely Heart was murdered—as if anybody cared—prove it, swear to get the killer. You had to shoot off your big mouth about Pop. You had to have hunches.

So now you're the patron saint of the Lonely Hearts Club, including a medal and a flood of useless hysterical publicity. Now you've got the Commissioner down on your neck. Julie's mad at you. The other sheets have got you pegged as the dean of news phonies and *Printer's Ink* comes up with: "For readers who like their stories as drummed-up bunko, Mr. McCleary may well constitute their best entertainment; but for those who think otherwise, he will constitute a monumental bore."

It isn't the case of Lonely Heart any more. It's McCleary vs. the police, press and public—to say nothing of the slayer. And a present from the Press Club: a small tin figure—*tin*, mind you, McCleary— of a skinny, fig-leafed Adonis complete with halo, spreading wings, Adam's apple and motto: "Ambassador of Suckers."

He sank lower in the chair. One week, to do this to me, one stinking little week. A nightmare beginning with that streamer: SLAYER THREATENS McCLEARY.

Sure, he had raised hell about that. It had scared Julie sick, too. But what could he do?

And then that crowd of Lonely Heart Club members who had charged into the city room, surrounding him and swearing to rally to his support, protect him. And the speech he had to make, with Biddle taking pictures. Lance felt his ribs tenderly; he could still feel the dent where the fat Swede, No. 239, had hugged him. Two ex-pugs had turned up as his bodyguards—hired by Carl, with Biddle taking pictures. That son-of-a-gun, Carl. . . . "Come here, Lance, I want to show you something."

He had led Lance into Madison's office and taken a revolver out of his pocket. Madison squealed. Lance remembered his own bright remark, "Fourth of July we got now. A new angle, Mr. Madison."

"Paid ten dollars for it in a hockshop this morning,"

Carl said. "Ten dollars. In two seconds it's going to spell ten thousand copies."

And he had fired through the window. Madison screamed. That was the only laugh, Madison's screaming. Carl had picked up the phone, been connected with headquarters, the Commissioner's office. "This is Chapman of the *Comet*. The killer of Lonely Heart and Pop Farnsworth just took a shot at Lance McCleary. In the publisher's office. No, missed him . . ."

And Biddle had come in with his camera and taken more pictures.

Then the break, colorfully written, boldly presented: he was to meet the killer at high noon on Times Square, to show himself in the open. By that time he was hypnotized; so he had gone to Times Square. But so had fifty million Club members, and the cops had to be called out, with Biddle taking pictures.

Pictures—pictures . . . His face frontpaged daily and plastered on the walls week ends. "I'm using roto for Saturday supplement," Carl said—and the christening of that section took place with a full-page picture of the great McCleary.

I'm so sick of my pan I could . . . I'm sick of this whole damn business. It's making an old man out of me. Julie's right. Then why don't I bow out? What am I waiting for? By God, I will—right now.

Feeling tremendously light of soul, mind and body, he rose and walked to the city desk. And there was another picture of him, captioned: NEXT VICTIM?

That's the topper. "Carl, I want to be yanked off this story."

Carl put his elbows on the arms of his chair, interlocked his fingers over his stomach. "Why?"

Lance thumped the picture angrily. "That's why! How long did you think I'd take this tin-horn show on the chin?"

Carl laughed. "What have you got to kick about? I'm making you a personality. The *Sun* had O'Malley, the *World* had Cobb, now the *Comet's* got McCleary."

"In installments! You can write 'the end' to that serial as of now."

Carl shrugged. "We've got a world-beater. I hate to see you take the count on it. It's a story that comes once—"

"What story? What've we got? Show me what we got and I'll pound the mill for twenty hours without a stop. But what've we got? Nothing!"

"So you want to be yanked off?" said Carl slowly.

"I'm no quitter. If I had something—something to work on . . ."

"You mean you still think you can dig up something?"

He's looking at me as if he were testing me. Lance felt a twinge of panic. I got to let him know I'm through—but through. "Hell, no. Call off your dogs or get yourself another Charlie McCarthy. Lonely Heart can stay lonely. I'm washed up with her!"

BOOK THREE

Twenty-Two

Lance was so bored, his eyeballs ached. He looked around the rectory for one—just one—congenial soul who spoke his language. He was the only outsider among the guests at Mabel's wedding.

He slunk to a corner, hugged the wall and counted the minutes until he could escape. He had promised Julie to be patient until she caught the bouquet.

A great laugh rang across the room. He instantly hated the cheer-bearer. Anybody who laughed like that was a false alarm. A thick hearty Irish brogue went with the laugh. He heard it closer to him. Julie pulled at his arm.

"This," she said, "is Mr. McCleary, Father."

Strong fingers closed over his own. He winced, withdrew a paralyzed hand, stared into the smiling eyes of the priest. Broad-shouldered, broad-faced, broad-beamed, the two-hundred-and-seventy pounder was bearlike, ruddy, a good inch taller than he.

"Aye," boomed Father Campion. "I knew it the minute I laid eyes on him."

Lance resented him. Most of these guys who walked around with a big smile, a hearty laugh, a glad hand, were never on the level. Like that brawny con man he once interviewed.

"McCleary . . ." The priest chewed the name carefully. "I know a Brian McCleary of Donaghadee whose ancestor followed the Rapderrey chief. He was courting Biddy Toole . . . Last I heard of him they were celebrating their seventh, a boy." His eyes twinkled. Blue, strong, clear. "I've heard a great deal of you, McCleary."

Another subscriber . . . "Read the *Comet*, eh?"

"No, son." Lance scowled at the "son." "What I heard of you was from this lass—'fair as flowers on the lea, she's neat and complete from neck to knee.' She tells me you're a newspaperman."

"Yeah."

"I've met many in your craft, McCleary, many. A great number of them are happily married."

Lance smiled inwardly. Julie was taking no chances. She must have told him to get to work on me. I'll give him a run for his money. "Ever hear of Professor Bailey?"

"Can't say that I have, lad."

"He's the first sociologist who tackled the Holy Writ from a modern point of view."

"Indeed? And how's that?"

"He translated 'Good Samaritan' as 'good sport'— 'wise virgins' as 'smart girls'—'laying up a treasure' as 'making a pile'—'repent' as 'get wise to yourself'—"

"Mr. McCleary!" cried Julie, shocked.

"Made page one with it. Called miracles 'the breaks.'" Lance waited for prompt denunciation. There was none.

The priest shrugged good-naturedly. "Some people like very low burlesque."

Julie glared at Lance indignantly. He was glad when she was called away. She threw him a sharp glance that was unmistakable: Behave yourself!

"Tell me, son," said the priest. "What is it you have against the wedding ring? Afraid?"

So we're back to that. "Look, Father, instead of shilling for Julie, why don't you—" He decided against that, changed to, "What part of Ireland you from?"

"Tralee."

"My grandfather was the rambler from—"

"Clare."

"How'd you know?"

"Sure and everybody knows of Terry McCleary, the rambler from Clare, who fought in Rathreale. He was captured and five hundred strong broke the jail door to free him."

"So it's not a hopped-up yarn."

"Just as hopped-up as Tinkers-to-Evers-to-Chance."

"Oh—you go for baseball, Father?"

"That I do."

"The fights?"

"Aye . . . and I could tell you—" Father Campion looked over his shoulder guiltily. "But this isn't the time or place, is it?"

Hey, I'm beginning to like this guy. "Anything you want—"

"I'd only be too glad, son." The priest rapped a knuckle into Lance's stomach and nodded in the direction Julie had taken. "You've known her three years, lad, and it would give me pride and joy to have you both stand up before me."

"Maybe I'm not the marrying kind."

"Och, McCleary! 'Tis ashamed I am of you."

"How long has she been touting you—I mean giving you this song-and-dance?" grinned Lance.

"One year come this All Saints' Day."

"Why, the little—"

The priest chuckled. "McCleary, you haven't got a chance. Why don't you set the day here and now?"

Lance gave up. "Don't you ever get fed up marrying people?"

"Och, no. 'Tis my greatest happiness."

"I mean going through the same old routine, the same words, the same responses, the same—"

"But it's never the same, lad. Each couple is individual."

Lance was skeptical. "How many of them have you hitched up?"

"Ho—Now you've got me. I'd have to look up my records. Quite a list, son, quite a list."

"Okay, I'll make a bet with you. You say each couple is individual. Well, you take that list—and I bet there won't be twenty-five you remember."

Suddenly, the wedding party ceased to exist. Lance did not hear them, see them. He stood in a vacuum staring at the priest.

"What's the matter?" asked Father Campion.

"I don't know . . . What'd I just say?"

The priest looked worried. "You were making a bet, son," he said soothingly. "About my not remembering—"

"That's it!"

"You'd lose the bet, m'boy."

"Talk some more!" prodded Lance urgently. "*Why* should I lose it?"

Father Campion was puzzled, but he went on. "It would take a bit of recalling—but if I had my records in front of me 'twouldn't be long before I'd be able to tell you at least a scrap about each couple."

"Suppose you had a picture."

"Oh, then 'twould be easy."

"How far back?"

Father Campion looked at him quizzically. "What are you getting at, son?"

I'm into something. I know it. Lance went closer to the priest. "Look, Father, if I showed you a picture of a man and woman married in the summer months of 1920, would you know them?"

"If they were on my records."

"But that's *twenty* years!"

The priest laughed. "I'm sorry we didn't make that bet."

"Julie!" shouted Lance. "Julie!"

She flew to his side, outraged at his causing a disturbance.

"Julie, can you get a list of every priest, rabbi, minister and justice of the peace in Massachusetts?"

She stiffened. "Have you been drinking?"

"This is important, honey. *Can you?*"

"Yes!"

"Good. Then as soon as this shindig's over—"

"Mr. McCleary, this is *not* a shindig."

"All right, all right. Kiss the bride for me."

Her hand clamped down on his arm. "Mr. Mc-Cleary, *where are you going?*"

"Back to the office. I've got work to do."

She flushed. "But you promised—"

She wasn't going to *cry?* "Look, honey, you want me to be happy, don't you?" he pleaded hastily. "How long is it since you've seen me happy?"

He had her there. "You black-hearted Irishman," murmured Father Campion softly.

"What work do you have to do all of a sudden?" asked Julie.

"Lonely Heart."

"But you said you were through with that!"

"New lead. *He* gave it to me." Father Campion looked startled. Lance pumped the priest's hand. "You're a prince, Father. So long. We'll get together sometime."

"Before the altar?" suggested Father Campion slyly.

I didn't hear that one, thought Lance hurrying out.

Cap'n Dickey was hunched over the wheel of his cab glumly enjoying the funnies.

"Comet," Lance told him, and leaned back. He hadn't felt so alive in weeks. The McCleary luck was holding out, after all. He loved Julie for dragging him to the wedding, he loved Father Campion, he even loved Mabel. He took out a cigarette, forgot to light it. He was thinking furiously, happy that a dozen angles came to him, fast, that he could pick and choose. I'd like to see the head in forty-eight point Kabel bold. Look good. Maybe even extra bold. They've got a lot of ultra Bodoni in stock. Look good, too. He knew exactly what he would write.

All he had to do was roll the copy paper into his typewriter; the lead wrote itself.

AN APPEAL

Do you remember this couple?

They were married in Massachusetts in the summer of 1920.

She is dead. She was murdered.

She is still unidentified.

We are looking for the man in this picture—her husband.

The police are looking for him.

We want your aid.

We believe the husband is the murderer.

He has added another victim to his list.

He is at large and dangerous.

Did you perform the wedding ceremony?

Look at their faces. Study them. Are they familiar? Try to remember. Look into your records.

If you have any information please write or wire:

NEW YORK *Comet.*

He ripped it from the machine and took it over to Carl. The old spring is back in your knees, McCleary.

"Know what we are, Carl?" he said. "Dopes."

"Why don't you talk louder so the copy boys can tell me what *they* think of me?"

"All right, *I'm* the dope."

"Now you can talk loud."

"Right under our noses and we didn't see it."

Carl yawned. "Now I'm supposed to say what—so I'll say it: What?"

"The only way to bust Lonely Heart wide open—"

"Are we back on that? Thought you were washed up."

"So did I—until a half hour ago."

"What've you got now—*two* fat bums waiting outside?"

Wise guy. I'll make him quit horsing. "How would you like to meet the guy who married Mr. and Mrs. Lonely Heart?"

"How would I like to own this paper?"

"Well, here's your introduction." Lance slapped the appeal down on the desk.

Carl read it. "Very touching. What'd they serve at that wedding?"

"Oh, for Pete's sake, Carl, don't you get it? We take that picture of them, make a billion copies, attach that to each one and shoot 'em out to every priest, minister, rabbi, justice of the peace in Massachusetts! *One* of them'll connect. We'll sign Julie's name to it —Religious Editor'll get them."

Ah—now Carl doesn't think I'm just playing straight man. I've got him sitting up. He knows it's a good idea, damned good.

"Hate to be licked, don't you, Lance?" said Carl.

"It's a natural. We'll get somewhere with this. And with the clergy behind us, how can we miss? They'll spout about the *Comet* from their pulpits. We'll have every church endorsing the move. We're a cinch for a jump. That's what you want, isn't it?"

What's the matter with him? I thought he'd grab this. What's he waiting for? "Hey, Carl, are you listening?"

Carl nodded. He was looking at the appeal. "It's been twenty years," he said.

Oh, that. "That's nothing. Should have told you. Priest I met at the wedding said with his records to help him, he could remember every couple that stood up in front of him. And we got a picture!"

"Maybe he's dead . . ."

"Who—the baby who performed the ceremony? It's worth taking that chance, isn't it?"

Why's he taking so long about the O.K.? We got nothing to lose.

Carl raised his head. "All right. I'll do it."

Oh, now it's *I*. When I was taking the rap it was *we*. Lance grinned. "Can I come home?"

"Yes," said Carl. "All is forgiven."

Twenty-Three

It was late. A janitor pushed a paper-filled crate through the city room. A scrub woman near the rewrite desks was lowering herself gingerly to her knees. Carl was alone at his desk.

His last conference with the circulation manager had assured him that the million mark could be reached with one more loaded run. Madison, usually timid and nervous, had been surprisingly mellow and optimistic. The only sour note had been from the business manager—a minor tempest because the reward for the killer had reached an outlandish sum. Carl chuckled.

He had announced the final abandonment of Lonely Heart. They had asked him what substitute he would use and he had smiled coolly as if he knew. But he did not. He was faced now with the interlude in which he must find a new heroine or hero or cause to keep the *Comet* the readers' delight as its seemingly uncanny prescience linked headlines with red-hot, unpredictable news. With Lonely Heart scrapped, circulation would drop. It was amazing—after all this time people wanted more of her. He could make them forget her. But he would have to plaster page one with a new play immediately. What?

He studied page two layout of the Bulldog dummy: the results of a cruel traffic in imbecile girls released from asylums and hired by employers looking for cheap help. Not bad . . . The girls worked for little or no money, were thrown on the street when they were no longer useful. Some became prostitutes, some married—their own kind. The children they produced were feeble-minded.

It was a good story. It had heart-punch. It was an exposé. He could inveigle leading psychiatrists, trumpet a crusade for unfortunate children, initiate a ban on indiscriminate habeas corpus. But it was distasteful. Besides, morons became monotonous. Madness was good. Madness, murder, mystery. But this story—every other sheet would have full coverage on it by the next edition. No, he'd have to let it go on the blind page.

He stretched tired arms, linked his fingers behind his head. Ave atque vale, Lonely Heart. What a shot in the arm Lance's idea had been. He could so easily have flared with impatience at Lance for wanting to give life again to a story he, the editor, had let die. He could have stopped Lance once and for all, then and there. And he would have . . . except that he knew he had nothing to fear.

They had stopped off at the town of Franklin to be married, had gone on, one of the many couples who passed through. How long had the ceremony taken: five minutes, ten? No, she would never be recognized.

He smiled at the scrub woman who had scraped her

pail along the floor and was ducking apologetically for making such a noise. Poor Lance; he had given the paper an additional twenty-thousand run; that had been his alibi for reopening the story. But actually, Carl knew, he was burning to redeem himself and come to the end of the trail with the unmasking of the killer.

Carl had turned the whole thing over to him. How Lance had strutted—and how he had wilted. With popular hysteria slowly stimulated, the results had been hysterical. He had watched Lance snowed under an avalanche of letters, all of them false—as Carl had known they would be; stay at his desk in ten and twelve hour sessions to receive personally notes, wires, phone calls; to interview the host of informers, tipsters, racketeers, lunatics, seers, religious fanatics, who had marched through the city room to his desk; hammer at his typewriter with ever-increasing venom —and nausea.

Until Lance couldn't take it. He was punchy with fatigue, mental, moral, physical, his face drawn, his eyes dull and circled with shadow.

"Carl, I'm getting out of this—for good."

"We went over this once before. You wanted it killed and I killed it. Then you come in with a brainstorm and I played ball with you. Now when we've got the ball rolling, you want me to kill it again."

"I know, I know. But this time I'm down for the count. Make me hunting and fishing editor. Put me in charge of the junior-fliers' page."

"My, you sound pathetic, Mr. McCleary. But okay, I'll let it peter out slowly. Meanwhile—"

"Nope. I'm ditching crime. I promised Julie that if I didn't pan out on this yarn we'd get married. That's what I'm going to do. I need a nice long rest."

"Well, well, well. Congratulations. In three weeks you'll be hungry for Centre Street."

"In three weeks I'll be nature editor leading a butterfly expedition on the Palisades!"

That had been that afternoon. Carl glanced at his watch. Rose would be getting worried. Ten to one, at this moment, Lance was very very drunk. Or had Julie decided not to take a chance and hauled him straight off to a priest. No, she'd demand—and get— a large wedding. I must tell Rose to start looking around for a wedding present.

He heard footsteps through the city room. The janitor had gone. Lance came into the light, dropped into a chair.

"What's the matter? Battle with the bride?"

"She's no bride yet," said Lance. "I must have walked around the block ten times before I figured out an angle."

"On what? How to save on the ring?"

Lance didn't smile. "Didn't know you were still here. Dropped in to leave it on your desk so you'd see it first thing in the morning."

"Something good?"

"The happy ending," said Lance quietly.

What was the matter with the boy? It wasn't like him not to shout when he had something important enough to drag him back to the office at this hour. "Well, don't keep it a secret. What is it?"

Lance handed him a sheet of paper. Carl unfolded

it, leaning forward to catch more light. It was a
letter. He caught the signature: "Harvey A. Miller—
Justice of the Peace."

Miller? Justice of the Peace? Five words at the top
of the letter leaped up at him: *83 Penn Avenue,
Franklin, Massachusetts.*

83 Penn Avenue . . . They had walked up the
path to the small yellow house and banged the brass
knocker twice. Miller had opened the door, a meek
little man with a knob of a head and gold-rimmed
spectacles.

>   83 Penn Avenue,
>   Franklin, Massachusetts.

Julie Allison,
Religious Editor,
New York *Comet,*
New York.

Dear Miss Allison:—

I can identify the couple in the picture you sent me
accompanying your appeal for help. I performed the
wedding ceremony. I am willing to cooperate and
help you and the police in any way I can.

Even though it's been twenty years, I know this
is the same couple because she came to me when she
got in trouble and I tried to help her. It was such a
sad story.

>   Yours truly,
>   Harvey A. Miller
>   Justice of the Peace.

The sheet made a tiny crackling sound. His hands
were trembling. He folded them one over the other

on the desk. But his knuckles were white with the effort. He leaned back so that his hands could be on his lap out of sight. "What else?"

"That's it, Carl."

Lance isn't excited. He's quiet. Because he's sure. He knows this is the link. I must be impatient. "Lance, it's just another one of those letters. A come-on."

"No. Not this one."

Fury pinned Carl to his chair, choked his throat. He heard his own voice, firm, unperturbable. "You've read too many of them. You're confused." He tore the letter in half, dropped it into his empty wastebasket.

Lance said nothing. He reached down, pulled the basket to him and lifted the pieces out.

Carl's temple began to throb. "What the hell, Lance!"

Lance fitted the letter together. "Look, Carl, this guy isn't asking for any dough. He doesn't want any-thing. He just says he can identify them. Look at that line: 'She came to me when she got in trouble.' That line's got something. It broke me and Julie up. I was all set to walk down the aisle, when I spotted it."

Damn his persistence. "I'm not arguing with you— it's late, I'm tired, Rose is waiting for me—I'm telling you: the story's cold. I wouldn't even squeeze that into the blind page."

"You won't have type big enough to handle it," Lance murmured.

"Talking to yourself? I just told you I scrapped it!" Careful. My voice broke. No, he'll think I'm angry. That's all right.

"Don't get sore. It's not going to cost us a fortune. We can follow-up and—"

"Forget it!"

"I can't."

"Why not?" Did I shout then?

"Not until you make out a voucher for twenty bucks to me."

"What for?"

"Railroad fare." Lance was solemn. "I wired Miller the twenty in your name to come here."

Twenty-Four

The dawn was slow in coming. Carl caught himself willing the sun to rise. He flung an arm over his tortured eyes. I'm out of my mind.

Beside him, Rose was breathing quietly, deep in the last profound sleep before the coming of day. She did not stir.

Oh, Rose, *if I could only talk to you.* I'm frantic. I don't know what to do. I've been trying to think. All through the night, while you thought I was asleep, I've been thinking. I hate the night! Those are the worst times—the nights. . . .

Miller is coming. Do you know what that means? He'll walk into the city room, straight to me, and point, and shout, "That man is John Grant!"

No. What's the matter with me? That's not it. He wouldn't recognize me. How could he? I've changed in twenty years, my voice, my manner. No mustache now. I've filled out.

That's not the danger. It's John Grant. *There must be no one alive who connects John Grant with Lonely Heart.*

I wanted to fly there tonight. That was my first idea. But how do I know he isn't on the way down? And if he isn't—whom does he live with? How could I break in at night?

But he will say the names—Charlotte Faith and John Grant. The police will check public records; people I have forgotten will come forward with whatever they know. And Lance . . .

Rose—I am afraid of Lance. He is so clever, so stubborn, so painstaking. He'll go to Worcester. He'll take it step by step; he'll piece things together. He'll never give up. He'll track me down until he knows that John Grant is Carl Chapman.

Oh, God, why did I change my name? Just to escape *her*, to lose myself in the world . . . But if I had not—*think*, Rose, *if I had not* . . .

The blackness after the first gray false dawn was fading before the sun. If he could only rise. But then he would waken Rose. There would be solicitous questions, alarm. He could only hold himself rigid and wait. . . .

The mail was on his desk when he got to it. He shuffled through the envelopes, quickly. There it was, the airmail letter postmarked Franklin, Mass. It was addressed to him. It was brief.

83 Penn Avenue,
Franklin, Massachusetts.

Carl Chapman,
City Editor,
New York *Comet*,
New York.

Dear Mr. Chapman:—

Received the twenty dollars you sent me to come to New York. I am unable to leave my home. Shall I

mail my information to you, or do you prefer to have
your representative come to see me?

> Yours truly,
> Harvey A. Miller
> Justice of the Peace.

P.S. Am enclosing the twenty dollars. My purpose
in helping you is not a mercenary one.

The twenty was in one bill. Carl tore the letter into
shreds. He was shaking with exhilaration. He need not
have feared . . . This is my chance. He can't come
here. I'll be that representative. I'll get him
alone. . . .

It was 9:10 now. He called the airline. A plane was
leaving for Boston at 9:45. He could make it. He
would arrive at 11.

It was four miles to Franklin from Boston. He paid
off the cab driver and walked to Penn Avenue.

Still lined with elms. It had not changed. Exactly
from this corner he had driven down the street with
Charlotte to the yellow house. But he was not dis-
turbed by reminiscences. He was calm. His mind had
never been more clear.

He walked up the path to the house. The brass
knocker was still on the door. He glanced up and
down the street. Empty. No one saw him. He lifted the
knocker, let it fall.

The door was opened by a small wrinkled bundle
in a wheel chair. It had a knob head and gold-rimmed
spectacles. What was left of Judge Miller peered up at
him.

"Judge Miller?"

"Yes?"

"I'm from the New York *Comet*."

"Oh. Come in . . . Go right into the parlor." The judge twisted his chair expertly.

The square piano was in the same corner, two miniatures on the wall above it. He had not thought of this room in twenty years, he had not been conscious of it that day; it amazed him that he could recall every detail . . . the spinning-wheel, the collection of walking sticks, the Colonial chair, the worn sofa, the Bible on the table, the flowerless brown vase.

"Sit down—sit down."

He sat on the sofa. Miller manipulated the chair to face him.

"You're alone?" said Carl.

The judge sighed. "All alone. Lost my wife seven years this Sunday. Did Mr. Chapman get the twenty dollars all right? I don't trust money in the mail."

"I'm Chapman." Why wait? He's helpless. I can get it over with quickly.

"Oh—the boss . . . Your work must be so interesting, Mr. Chapman. I have often thought—"

"Do you mind—?" Carl forced himself to smile. "I have to get back to the paper."

"Yes, yes, of course." The judge wheeled to the table. From the Bible he took the appeal and photograph that had been sent to him, Lance's telegram. Beside the Bible was a thick ledger. He patted it. "My records. Would you like some lemonade? Always keep a pitcher of it in the icebox. I can't make it as good as my wife used to. She'd always know just how much sugar to put in it."

"No thanks; I'm not thirsty. Do you know the names of the couple in that picture?"

"Sure do. Got the record of their marriage right here in this book. John Grant and Charlotte Faith. Odd for a surname—Faith. Grant came from Worcester. She was a Provincetown girl."

How would a hoodlum attack? Probably with one of those walking sticks. It would be simple. "So they were strangers in Franklin?"

"That's right."

"You must have married a great number of them—strangers, I mean."

"Oh, yes."

"But you're sure that couple is Mr. and Mrs. John Grant."

"As sure as I'm Harvey Miller."

"You must have a sharp memory to be able to place strangers after twenty years."

"I couldn't forget her face, Mr. Chapman. She was such a pitiful character. So sad. Want to take notes?"

Cause: Robbery . . . "You say they're in your book?" He got up.

The judge opened it, pointed to the entry. It was in July. There were other names . . .

"Does anyone else know he's John Grant?"

"Why, no. I knew you would want it to be—exclusive." The judge beamed, proud of himself.

I'll use the black cane in the corner. It's heavy; the

head is solid. . . . He took a step toward it. "In
your first letter you mentioned that she came to you
when she was in trouble. What did you mean by
that?"

"Poor woman, she thought I could help her. She was
almost crazy. You see, Mr. Chapman, he deserted
her. She got the idea that I could get him back since
I had brought them together as man and wife."

Another step. I must be cautious. I must give him
no chance to call out. "What did you do?"

"I went to the Missing Persons Bureau and put it
up to them. I could walk then. They sent out word—
but it was no use."

I was too clever for them.

"She told me the whole story. Oh, Mr. Chapman,
if you could have heard her, it would have wrung
your heart. She tried to take her life. She sold everything . . ."

*Even those blue wine glasses you always liked. I
had to find you.*

You never will.

"She had no one to help her. She was so lonely.
That's why she came to me . . ."

It was terrible, John. I was lonely. Oh, so lonely.

"She couldn't believe that he had really left
her . . ."

*I had to find out why you ran off. I had a right to
know. I must know.*

Because I hated you. I still hate you.

"When I tried to reason with her, she couldn't
seem to understand . . ."

Understand? You're still my husband.

The elevated roared by, the gnashing of wheels against rails vibrating through the room.

We're married. We're married. I'm your wife.

No, Charlotte, no.

"It was so pathetic. Through it all she kept one thing—her wedding ring . . ."

The light caught on the gold . . . *There was one thing I wouldn't pawn!* Her eyes accused him. *You couldn't get a divorce.*

I thought you were dead.

We took an oath. "Til death do us part."

Shut up, Charlotte!

I'm your real wife.

Stop it, Charlotte!

I'll tell them who you really are.

I won't let you!

I'll tell them about the woman you're living with!

He lunged at her. *I'll tell—I'll tell.* He got his hands around her throat. She fell backward. She writhed and tried to pull his hands away. He closed them tighter —tighter . . . Die, Charlotte, die . . .

She was dead. He could let go.

The shattering roar of a passing train filled his ears. His ear drums rang. Then there was silence . . .

He could hear again. He could see. A big book was on the floor . . . an overturned wheel chair . . . He stared at them in bewilderment.

That's Judge Miller dead on the floor!

He sprang back. It was *he* I killed? I thought it was Charlotte . . . He was caught by terror. What happened to me?

The truth rocked him. It left him cold, turned to

stone. His head ached. His eyes smarted. His fingers
were numb.

Am I . . . ? He would not admit the word. How
could I be? I am myself. I have intelligence. I can
see, think, feel, hear. I realize what I have done. I
came here to kill a man and I killed him.

But that wasn't I who did it. It wasn't *he* I killed.

When had he lost that authority, that possession
of himself that was Carl Chapman? He couldn't remember. All the rationalizing he had rehearsed had
failed him.

It was the strain I have been under, fatigue . . .
they took advantage of me . . . But he knew he was
excusing himself. Rage blinded him, and self-con-
tempt. He had been betrayed by weakness, who had
always despised weakness.

A factory whistle hooted shrilly. A distant church
clock boomed. He counted the strokes. Twelve. Noon.

He had no time now. Suspicions, self-accusations,
explanations—he would clear them later.

Now there was work to do. . . .

Twenty-Five

" 'When in the City of New York any person shall die by criminal violence or by casualty or by suicide or suddenly when in apparent good health or when unattended by a physician or in prison or in any suspicious or unusual manner . . .' "

Lance reread the lead of the feature he had done on Dr. O'Hanlon for the Saturday supplement. An old trick, opening with a dark and dramatic quote. He ran through the rest of the copy. Same old stuff: attitude of Medical Examiner toward his work, unique cases, irrefutable findings, valid conclusions, autopsies performed at white heat, crimes analyzed . . .

He dropped it on the city desk. "Everything's in there, Carl, but the water hose and Needle Nellie. May have added a slab or two."

Carl spiked the feature.

Lance loitered. "Say, Carl, it's been five days since I wired that judge a double saw-buck."

"As you've told me for the sixty-seventh time," said Carl, annoyed. "What do you want *me* to do? I haven't heard from him."

"Maybe he didn't get it yet."

" 'Maybe he didn't get it yet!' You know he pocketed it."

"Yeah. How about my twenty?"

"Ask Madison."

"Ah, come on now, Carl."

Carl jammed a batch of copy into the hand of a waiting boy. "Actually, you should stand the loss. No one gave you permission to wire a fraud twenty dollars. But I'll put a voucher through for you."

Lance grumbled back to his typewriter. He felt like the legman on his first beat who came back with everything but the facts. That letter from Miller had smacked of authenticity. He could recall it verbatim. But what about that twenty? Miller must have received it. And pocketed it. Just another run-of-the-mine reward racketeer with a fresh slant on a stale angle.

Forget it, McCleary. Just a bum guess on your part. He chewed a fingernail. But—it didn't smell con no matter what Carl said.

He stared at his phone. Why not? He picked it up, asked for long distance, and put through a call to Judge Harvey A. Miller in Franklin, Massachusetts—collect.

Franklin spoke. "Sorry, you can't get through to Judge Miller."

"Okay," snapped Lance, *"I'll* pay for it."

"That's not it, sir. Judge Miller is dead."

He almost smothered the phone. "What's that?" She repeated, "Judge Miller is dead."

Holy smoke. "Give me your police department." Four clicks . . . incongruous gabble . . . A gruff voice at the other end of the line made sense: "Sheriff Burt speaking."

Lance twisted his mouth. "This is Sergeant Pike, New York Police, Headquarters."

There was a gulp. He could almost see the sheriff swallow his tobacco. The gruff voice was not so gruff now.

"Yeah, sergeant?"

"What about Miller?"

"Choked to death."

Lance choked on that. He covered the transmitter. "Carl," he called, "Miller's been knocked off."

Carl didn't lift his eyes from his work. "How do you know?"

"Got Franklin police on the phone. I'm Sergeant Pike."

He saw Carl sweep up a phone. "Cut me in on McCleary."

Lance covered his right ear, closed his eyes. Carl's twang was perfect. "This is Commissioner Seanaman. Who's this?"

More tobacco swallowed by the sheriff. "Burt— Sheriff Burt, Mr. Commissioner."

"How did you say Miller was killed?" said Carl.

"Choked."

Lance made it a three-way conversation. "When?"

"Four days ago. They found him 'bout two in the afternoon. Slim Wilkins always plays checkers with th' judge an'—"

"Any clues?" barked Carl.

"Anything missing?"—Lance.

"What are you working on?"—Carl.

"Any suspects?"—Lance.

"Fingerprints?"—Carl.

"Enemies?"—Lance.

"Holding anybody?"—Carl.

"How'd it happen?"—Lance.

"*You* handling the case?"—Carl.

"Was he married?"—Lance.

The barrage tongue-tied the sheriff. He spluttered, managed to catch a foothold. "Robbed," he blurted. "Tramp must've done th' job. Watch taken. Place smashed up. Miller was a cripple, y'know, couldn't get outta his wheel chair. Easy to kill a cripple." He caught his breath. "What's up? New York lookin' for Miller?"

"Forget it," snapped Carl. "We just wanted to question him."

He and Lance hung up at the same time. They stared at each other. Lance threw out his hands.

"All right, all right," he shouted, "so I didn't get an okay for the phone call. Take it out of my salary."

Only four days ago Judge Miller had been alive, eager to cooperate, and now . . . Lance mooched along Times Square. Now what? *Now* if I go to Julie, she'll probably crack me over the skull. And I don't blame her.

"How you doin', Mac?"

He looked up from the sidewalk. Hoppe Fowler, maneuvering skillfully in front of his out-of-town newspaper stand, plucked a Denver *Post* from the Colorado rack and neatly slapped it under a customer's arm.

"H'lo, Hoppe," said Lance.

Hoppe gossiped about mutual friends. Lance listened absently. "Say, I got a new protégé, Mac. Young fella wants to be a reporter. Think you can fix it up for him with your boss?"

Lance scanned the Massachusetts rack. "What you got from Franklin?"

"He's only eighteen, willing to work—There's nine of 'em, Mac. Illinois, Kansas, Florida, Iowa, Massachusetts—"

"The one in Mass."

"*Gazette.*"

"What day?"

Hoppe plucked a few sheets from the rack. "Take your pick. Last one's about three days old."

Lance found a photo of Miller on page one. The *Gazette* had given him a one column cut and a full column on the funeral services, the clubs he had belonged to, the many couples he had married who attended the obsequies, the death of his wife, the accident that had crippled him, the vestments worn by the rector, the committal service, the stone, rectangular in shape, with its plain inscription, the will to be filed for probate. A stick on the robbery and strangulation was buried in the obituary.

"He's a great young fella," Hoppe said, "worked on his high-school paper—wants to be a columnist."

Lance caught a compact boxed yarn slugged: FRANKLIN CRIME WAVE. He read it carefully: "The robbery and outrageous murder of the incapacitated Judge Harvey A. Miller makes the second Franklin crime in four years. The first crime, committed four years ago, was the robbery of . . ."

Two crimes in four years . . . And one of them the murder of Judge Miller. . . . Why him? Robbery motive, they think. But he couldn't have been rich— a justice of the peace in a hick town. Why murder? To keep him from calling out? A good conk on the head would do that. He was strangled. How much of a fuss could a cripple in a wheel chair kick up? Yet the sheriff said the place was all smashed up.

"How about it, Mac?" said Hoppe. "He's only eighteen and a whiz when it comes to those big words."

"How far is Franklin from Boston, Hoppe? D'you know?"

" 'Bout four-five miles, I think."

Lance tossed the *Gazette* back into the rack.

"Hey," Hoppe yelled after him, "it's only a nickel!"

Twenty-Six

Lance found the Franklin *Spy* stabled in an ancient
two-story house of unrecognizable period. In front of
it, surrounded by ill-kept grass, was a weather-beaten
statue of a Liberty Boy. On the big plate glass window: MOSES BRADFORD, Editor and Proprietor.

The editorial office, one room, was deserted. He
knew these country papers from reading about them.
Once he had even toyed with the idea of working on
a small town weekly and becoming part of the oddest
organization in journalism—the Grass Root Press.

An antique flat-bed press was in the center of the
floor. He had once seen a picture of just such a press
in the Encyclopaedia Britannica. A roll-top desk had
innumerable pigeon holes, all choked with dusty
notes. Type was scattered. An order for a new font
was covered with ink smudges. A big pile of advertising electrotypes was heaped near three or four sets of
type cases, a proof press, some galley racks. Empty cans
of printer's ink were buried in cobwebs. A stairway
led up to unimaginable regions. But what surprised
him—it was out of place in the shop—was a genuine
linotype machine, "Mergenthaler 1902." Probably

bought on the installment plan, with fifty more years to pay off.

On the wall was a long yellow page, framed. In bold face the topline read: DOWN WITH THE STAMP ACT. He stepped closer to it. It was a page of the Franklin *Spy*, April 18, 1765; under the headline were the words: "Doom's-Day Number." A thrill ran down his spine. He was struck by the black border, evidence of deep mourning, with the skull and cross-bones and the deep black words, "The Times Are Dreadful, Dismal, Doleful, Dolorous, and Dollarless."

Next to it was another framed page: May 3, 1775. Its topline: "Americans!—Liberty or Death!—Join or Die!"

"If you're that typewriter salesman," a voice cackled suddenly into his ear, "don't fuss 'round me today. Don't need no typewriter. Never use one. Get my copy out on th' linotype. Write straight at th' melter."

He turned. The man looked old enough to have written those headlines himself. He brushed by Lance, plopped into the ancient swivel chair in front of the roll-top desk and pushed up the cardboard visor that was tied around his head with a string. The telephone hung on a bracket. He yanked it to him.

"Gil?" he rasped into it. "Moses Bradford. Now lissen, Gil, I know you're tryin' your best to pay off that death notice but them thutty acres you been farmin' since—Hey? You're sendin' a sack of 'tatoes up today? Oh, a'right, Gil, that'll do. But no skimpin', mind."

He thrust the telephone from him and peered up

at Lance over his glasses. "You still here? Told you I ain't buyin'."

"Nobody's trying to sell you a typewriter, Mr. Bradford. I'm Lance McCleary of the New York *Comet*."

The editor grunted. Lance saw him as the printer's salty devil who never grew up. The old man shot out a long white cuff and studied the names, items, memos scribbled on it. Lance warmed to him. The old man crossed a name off the cuff and plunged into copy with a thick black pencil anchored to the phone by a dirty string.

"Y'*look* like one o' them typewriter salesmen," he clacked. "Shucks, they been fussin' 'round me for months. Say th' *Spy* makes more spellin' errors than any paper in th' county."

Intrigued, Lance could think of no comment to that. The old editor needed none; he went right on.

"Heck, th' *Spy* wouldn't be no real paper if it didn't have a few mistakes now 'n' then. Gives our readers somethin' to fuss over. New York paper, eh? Well, sit down, brother, sit down."

Lance drew up a cracked leather chair. I'll mellow him up first. "Ever hear of the Draft Riots of 1863?"

Bradford nodded, spat; a brown stream crossed Lance's vision, landed neatly in a handy spittoon. It was the first sign Lance had that Bradford kept a wad of tobacco in his cheek.

Lance told him about Sweeney and Horace Greeley. When he was finished, Bradford lifted his head. "My father ran that story. July issue. Still got it in our

files. Fust Associated Press dispatch we ever used."
He leaned forward, tapped Lance's knee. "Don't
wanta call your friend Sweeney a liar, son, but in
that dispatch there was nothin' 'bout Greeley comin'
right out an' sayin' 'Save me, Johnny, save me!'"

Lance laughed. "Guess Sweeney stretches it a little
every time he tells it."

Bradford waggled his chin. "Now—what's on your
mind, young feller?"

"I'd like some information."

"Humph. Why don't y'ask th' *Gazette*. Some folks
think it's th' best paper in Franklin. Daily, y'know."

Lance smiled at the contempt in the old man's
voice. "I've been there, Mr. Bradford. The *Gazette's*
only ten years old—just a baby." That'll get him.
"They told me you've been putting the *Spy* to bed for
fifty years."

"Fifty-two an' never missed an edition."

"They said you know everything and anything
there is to know about this town."

The editor's bones creaked as he turned, studied
Lance shrewdly. "What kind of story you on, young
feller?"

Lance changed his mind instantly. He would not
show Bradford the photo of Mr. and Mrs. Lonely
Heart that he had in his pocket. Something—he
couldn't put his finger on it—told him not to take the
old man into his confidence. The Franklin *Spy* might
be a superannuated relic and Bradford an impotent
editorialist—but these cunning country editors with
their tricks and tobacco juice and ancient grasp of
news . . . Lance heard the danger bell, left the photo

untouched. Only a sucker shared a story with another newspaperman, no matter how harmless the colleague appeared.

"Human interest," he lied casually. "Special feature on marriages. Comparing Puritans, Quakers, Ozark natives. N.Y.U. professor claims New England marriages last longer, particularly in Massachusetts."

Bradford tugged at his right ear. "Don't believe a word of it," he snapped. "Pulled th' same hosstale on stilts m'self when I tried to fool th' editor of th' Fitchburg *News*. That was back in 1901. Big story that year —William Howard Taft became civil governor of th' Philippines. I needed confirmation, didn't want Henderson of th' *News* to know I was hep to it. Know what *I* told 'm? Said I was makin' a survey of trees."

He cackled, recalling the moment. "But don't let it worry you none, young feller. You tell your editor you put a slick one over on old Moses Bradford an' he'll give you a raise." He winked slyly. "What d'you say to that?"

"You got me against the wall. I'm on a yarn all right but I can't—"

A gnarled palm silenced him. Bradford plucked at a shaggy eyebrow, his eyes twinkling. "Yup, I know— can't share stories with rival papers, eh?" He straightened in his chair, rearranged his visor, adopted an air of executive impatience. "Let's git on with th' marriage assignment."

Lance produced a dozen names. "Got this list at the City Hall. Can you remember what happened to any of these couples?"

Bradford scanned the names. "Mm . . ." He shot a

look at Lance, that said: can I remember! "Picked 'em all in th' twenties, didn't you?" said the old man. "Nineteen-twenty, t'be exact."

Lance's heart jumped. Here before him was a font of information. He had taken a chance, selected names of couples married in the summer months of that year by Judge Miller. Now, with some luck . . .

"Mr. and Mrs. Max Paine," read off Bradford. "That one's easy. Max's runnin' a drug store now in Clinton at Maple an' Webb. Married Mehitabel Stevenson. Got himself a litter o' kids an'—"

"I don't suppose you've got pictures of them?" blurted Lance. Too late to recall the question. It had a pinch of sarcasm in it that he hadn't intended. He had once read that the shortest route to suicide is to remind a country editor that he couldn't afford his own cuts. He waited for the explosion.

It came. Bradford squinted, bristled, spat, swore, "Have we got pictures of 'em? This ain't no fortnightly rag, young feller. Know when photo-engravin' come into bein'?"

"No," said Lance meekly.

"1839," blasted Bradford, now red-faced. "Feller called Mongo Ponton. Thutteen years later Fox Talbot come out with that half-tone process." He grumbled to himself. "Do we have pictures . . ." He bellowed. "Had 'em since 1852!"

He spiked the copy he had slaughtered with vertical thick slashes and rose, bones creaking again. "Course we depend lots on boilerplate an' I ain't claimin' we run nothin' but zinc etchin's—but we manage to come out with half-tones even though *some folk* find it hard t'believe."

He started upstairs, halted, turned. "Well? Comin'?"

Lance followed him humbly up into a large room. He ducked a bulb dangling from the low ceiling. Shelves, jammed with bound copies of the *Spy*, surrounded them.

Bradford pulled out a frayed volume. "Keep 'em upstairs away from th' damp." He pointed to the issue dated April 15, 1865.

Lance saw one word: assassination.

"There's th' fust daguerreotype of Abe Lincoln," said Bradford, thumbing the picture. He shoved the book back, gripped Lance's arm, convoyed him over bundles of the *Spy*, still unbound. He tapped the first volume on the shelf. "That's when we fust saw light."

Lance, hypnotized, stared at the crudely printed numbers on the binding: 1721 . . .

For a moment he forgot everything. Carefully he pulled the musty birth of the *Spy* from its niche and opened it. A half-sheet folio, printed on only one side, with every line garbled; its printer and publisher: Zachariah Bradford. It took him a few moments to get used to the type. He made out something about white slaves, a plea for payment of subscriptions to follow and an account of a woman who had been hanged as a witch. ". . . The Divel that visited her was just of the same Stature, Feature, and complexion with what the Histories of the Witchcrafts beyond-sea ascribe unto him; hee was a wretch no taller than an ordinary Walking Staff; hee was not of a Negro, but of a Tawney, or an Indian color; hee wore a high-crowned Hat, with strait Hair; and had one Cloven Foot."

Bradford broke the spell. "Here it is, just as I said. Max married Mehitabel."

Lance gently pushed 1721 back, joined Bradford over an opened volume. He saw a two column photo of the Max Paines in a July issue of 1920. The screen wasn't half-bad.

"Lots o' strangers elope every year," said Bradford. "Come here t'get hitched. 'Course we don't bother none with 'em, only run pictures of couples who live here." He looked around for a place to spit, picked up a bundle of papers, spattered juice into a concealed cuspidor. "Too bad 'bout Judge Miller. He coulda helped you. He was robbed, choked t' death few days ago."

Lance complimented him on the screen. Bradford softened a little. He went down the list. First he re-traced his friendship with Jed Wilson who married Cynthia Everett, then he showed Lance their photo, the story. "See? Nice screen on 'em too, eh, young feller? Says Cynthia Everett. Never forget a name."

Next on the list were Mr. and Mrs. Raymond Greene. The old man raked up their past with a rich grunt. "Ray was a bad boy. Used t'read lots. Went to jail. Married Josie Aubry, French girl . . . Yup, busted right outta jail, clean smack out."

"What'd he do?"

"Used t'beat up Josie."

Lance became tense. "Where is he now?"

"Dunno. They put him away in that crazy house on Lincoln Avenue in Worcester. Busted right clean smack outta there, too."

Lance had to keep his voice down. "And you don't know where he is now?"

"Nope."

"Where's his wife?"

"Moved 'bout ten years ago."

"Let's see their picture."

Bradford pointed to it proudly. Lance studied Josie Aubry's features. She was not Lonely Heart.

Bradford went down the list, passing over the strangers to Franklin . . . Lance learned why Oliver Harndon opened a barber shop in Springfield; that Chris Phillips was killed in a lightning storm; how Guy Griscom found Mrs. Griscom in Chet Wilson's arms and what happened to Wilson.

At first he was amused at the way Bradford matched his memory against the names in the papers, but after nine couples he lost interest in the stories behind the stories of Franklin's Romeos and Juliets of 1920.

"Mr. and Mrs. John Grant," said Bradford. "Strangers." He passed them, went on to the next couple. "Mr. and Mrs. Ralph Barker—" He snapped his fingers. "Wait a minute, young feller, seems t'me I kinda recollect somethin' 'bout them Grants."

"Out-of-towners, you said."

"Yup. But she come back to Franklin fer somethin'."

"Look it up."

"Don't be in such an infernal hurry. Fust gotta

remember myself . . . John Grant." He ruminated. "John Grant . . . Charlotte. Sure. Charlotte. Desertion." He slapped his knee with gusto. "Desertion, young feller, or I ain't Moses Bradford. He left her high 'n' dry. She come back to th' only friend she had, Judge Miller. She had a picture of herself with her husband. Gave it to th' Judge. He slipped it to me an' I sent it to Boston. Three-column cut, young feller. Cost all of seven dollars, ninety-four cents." He nudged Lance in the ribs. "Nice beat, eh? None of th' other papers had th' desertion story—or th' picture."

She came to me when she got in trouble . . . . Have I got it at last? "Where's John Grant now?"

"Dunno."

"And the woman?"

"Dunno. Let me tell you somethin' about Ralph— Oh, here's that cut on th' Grants. Look at it. Right on th' front page. How d'you like *that* screen, young feller? Now, gettin' back to Ralph . . ."

Lance stared at the picture of Charlotte Faith and John Grant. There it was, on the front page of the *Spy*. It was the same picture he had in his pocket; the same one she had given to Judge Miller; the same one Bradford had sent off to Boston twenty years ago for a three-column cut; the same one found in Lonely Heart's suitcase . . .

Bradford watched him. He was proud. "Nice balance for page one, ain't it? Usually run 'em two columns but that desertion called for an extra. Worth seven-ninety-four just to get an exclusive on th' picture, eh?"

Lance stared at the caption under the photo of Mr. and Mrs. Lonely Heart in front of a flivver, a Just Married sign, old shoes and cans tied to a rear bumper:

MR. AND MRS. JOHN GRANT (CHARLOTTE FAITH) WHEN WEDDING BELLS RANG AND EVERYTHING WAS BLISS. . . .

Twenty-Seven

Rose had said the doctor would be there between five and six. It was five-fifty now and she hadn't called. Carl couldn't wait. He reached for the phone just as it rang.

From the first tones of her voice he knew Tommy was better. "It's a slight ear infection from his cold," she said. "Dr. Weller's just leaving."

Ear infection. *Mastoid*, he thought. But he was afraid to say the dread word. "Let me speak to him."

Dr. Weller's bland voice gave him no assurance.

"Look, Danny, give it to me straight," Carl ordered. His lips were stiff; he moistened them. "Don't let Rose hear, but *tell* me."

"You parents," the doctor laughed. "It's nothing, Carl. I told you. Rose has the drops for his ear. Just keep him warm and out of a draft. He can get out of bed in a couple of days."

Rose got back on the phone. "Stop worrying, darling."

He saw her as she had been that morning, bending over their son. His heart contracted with his love for her. He remembered little Edith, awestruck and frightened, tiptoeing out of the bedroom.

"Is it contagious?" he asked. "Keep Edith away from him."

Rose laughed. She gave him life with that laugh. "He's showing temper again. Isn't it wonderful? He just threw his Teddy Bear at me. I'm so happy."

"I'll buy him a new one. I'll buy him—"

"No, you don't. He's got enough. Don't you bring him any more toys!" How good it was to hear her scolding him. "Try to get home early, dear. You didn't get any sleep last night."

He hung up. He leaned back in his chair and stretched. Prindle, glancing up, caught his eye and smiled. I must have been grinning like a fool. But Prindle doesn't know how I feel. He hasn't any children. He doesn't know what it's like.

Twenty thousand dollars . . . The bonus was his; he would get it. He could break the million mark. And then—Miami. One solid month of it. Rose and he and Edith and Tommy. This year he would teach the kids to swim. They would have no fear with him holding them. Rose looked well in a bathing suit. They would live in their suits—in the sun, in the peace, in the quiet. He needed the rest.

Was he at the zenith of his career? He had Manhattan's highest paid stable of writers and deskmen without a fortune wasted on trained seals. He had jumped the value of the *Comet's* circulation, press franchises, libraries. He was close to the million circulation mark. Was this the top? And if it was, could he stay there?

He knew he was teasing himself, enjoying it—because he knew the answer. This is not the zenith. I can go higher . . .

"Charlotte Faith and John Grant."

I must stop. I must stop thinking aloud. Forget them. Drive them out of my mind. I'm through with all that.

"Didn't you hear me, Carl? I said Charlotte Faith and John Grant."

It wasn't me. Someone else said it. He looked up. Lance was grinning down at him.

I've gone through too much. I can't feel any more. Let me alone, Lance, let me alone.

"You don't know who I'm talking about, do you?" said Lance smugly. "Charlotte Faith and John Grant —Mr. and Mrs. Lonely Heart."

How does he know? It was hard to breathe. Carl opened his mouth.

Lance chuckled. "Floored you, didn't I? That's where I've been all day—Franklin. Had a hunch and ran up there. A cinch. City Hall opened up the books, an old guy who runs a weekly there opened up his files—" Lance spread his hands. "There they were, planted smack on page one, both of them. He deserted her."

This isn't happening. I'll go to Miami. The sun is warm there. I'll take Rose and the kids.

Lance put his hands flat on the desk and leaned forward. "Now I can get married. I licked the story." He was grinning again as he straightened. "Got all the dust since 1721 on me. Got to get a shower. See you later."

He started away. In a burst of enthusiasm, he blurted. "We're all set, Carl. All you've got to do is splash it all over the front page." His voice betrayed his self-satisfaction as well as conviction. " 'Who is John Grant? Where is John Grant?' We'll have him in twenty-four hours!"

Carl found himself staring at the spot where Lance's shoulders disappeared behind the row of lockers before the entrance. His eyes ached with staring.

I've got to get out of here.

He tried to push his chair back and sagged, clinging to the desk, his hand missing a spike by an inch. He crouched there, fighting a pain that forked over his eyes. He needed Rose. He wanted her near him to lay a comforting hand on his trouble. She never spoke much. She would say a quieting word and let a silence warm her reassurance.

But Rose could not help him now.

I've got to get out of here. He took a deep breath. *Now . . .*

He rose, took his hat off the tree, put it on. At the door he remembered, went back. He knew in which drawer it was. Someone shoved a proof under his nose and asked for an okay. He grunted. When he was alone he slipped the gun in his pocket and walked out of the city room.

He remembered another walk. South Street and the fish markets and the river and Keene's . . .

Help me. Help me, somebody, *help me.*

But he knew he had forfeited help.

He's like my son. Crazy, tall, redheaded boy, always in high good humor. Everything I learned I taught him. I learned from him too . . . Oh, God, not Lance. Not Lance!

Hoofs clattered past him. A small cavalcade of horse-drawn junkwagons on its way to the stables . . . Sullen antagonism suddenly flared into open hostility when one of the drivers was hard-pressed to the curb by a competitor. He lifted a furrowed mahogany face and cursed violently. "Gimme room, you bastard, or I'll kill yuh!"

It had been easy with Pop. First Charlotte, then Pop, then Miller. But they were strangers. Lance was Lance. Lance was his boy.

I can't do it.

With the thoroughness of a man groping through a nightmare he found himself circling Lance's block. Less than a block away was the *Comet*.

I can't do it.

There was just one thing to do. Clear out. Run. Get away. But where? I've got to think, got to think.

Not Lance. He's like my son. I can't touch a hair on his head. I love him as I'd love my own boy. What he doesn't know, I do; what he can't do, I can. To-gether we're one.

He walked down the street, the heavy death in his pocket, his fist over it. . . . He brooded. The pistol was an act of strong will. Behind that was the story of a lanky youth sent out on his first police assignment. Behind that was the friendship that grew between editor and reporter. Behind that was a harmony that cemented them together, he and his devoted arch foe.

He upbraided Lance for his dogged persistence. He

upbraided himself. "I know who she was." That was when I should have stopped it.

He paused in front of Lance's apartment house. A stubborn impenetrable wall between his conscience and the entrance barred his way. Why am I hesitating? The past I know should make this simple. I'm complicating it.

On the second floor he waited outside Lance's door. He heard the roar of the shower. He knocked and waited. Lance couldn't hear him. No one passed. When he had turned on the water for *her,* it had made little sound, just that steady trickling . . .

He no longer heard the shower. He knocked again. Lance let him in, a towel wrapped around his middle, his body pink with rubbing.

"What brings you here, Carl? Chow with me?"

"No."

Lance dressed quickly. "Then what? You didn't drop in to watch me dress." He winked. "Do we split the reward?"

"Who else knows about John Grant?"

Lance ducked to see himself in the mirror. "Hit the jackpot, didn't I?"

"Who else?"

"Told you. Just me."

"What about that weekly editor?"

"He thinks I was on a special feature stint. He didn't connect them with anything. Just kept on wading through the file."

"And the picture?"

"Same one we got. Smart boy, ain't I?"

"I wish you weren't! Anyone but you."

Lance stared at him in the mirror. "Why?"

"I've got to kill you, Lance."

"Huh?" Lance turned around quickly. Carl had a gun in his hand. It had been hidden by the rim of the mirror. It wasn't a fake; Lance had seen enough of them to know. "Hey—that's a real gun!"

"Six bullets."

"Whose is it?"

"Mine."

Then that was the same gun Carl had used to shoot the hole in the window . . . The damn fool! He doesn't need another exploitation stunt. We've got the McCoy. Doesn't he know that? . . . He's staring at me as if he really didn't see me. Who stares like that? Oh, yeah, that blind beggar on the corner. Carl's sick. He looks so old. I never noticed how gray he's gotten. He looks old enough to be my father.

Carl felt tears at the back of his eyes. Lance is frightened. That's how Tommy looks at me when he knows he has to be spanked . . . I mustn't hurt him. Let my hand be steady. Let me shoot him where it won't hurt, so that he'll die quickly.

"Stop pointing that at me!" snapped Lance.

"I'm going to kill you."

He's drunk. Carl's drunk! No, he isn't. He's sick. He's crazy. So calm—he's going to kill me. I've got to stall him . . . "Why me?"

He's stalling me. He thinks I'm mad. "Lance—I'm John Grant."

Oh, the poor guy. He's worked so hard. He's been too close to the story. No rest. He's all mixed up in his head. He thinks he's John Grant. When did he

snap? I've got to tell Rose. She must take him away.
"Take it easy, Carl."

"It's true, boy. You saw the story. I deserted her.
Changed my name. I was John Grant—Charlotte
Faith was my wife."

"No, Carl—Rose is your wife. Rose! Rose! Hang on
to that Carl!"

I must explain about Rose. "I didn't know she was
alive when I married Rose. She came back. She
threatened to expose me. I didn't care for myself,
Lance, believe me. But Rose, the kids . . . I killed
her. I didn't mean to, Lance."

Oh, the relief of being able to say it: I killed her.
The sweet sweet relief. I'll tell him everything. I'll
rid myself of it now—forever—and I'll be *free*. He'll
understand, he'll forgive—and with his death there
will be no remorse, no dread. Only blessed grief,
because he forgives . . . He is believing me at last.
His eyes are straining with horror.

"Then you killed Pop too . . ." whispered Lance.
"Yes."

The mouth of the pistol was a ring of light. Oh, no,
not Carl!

"Pop had the pawn ticket and you were afraid."

"Of you, Lance. I taught you too well."

"All the while you were making me the fall guy
you knew . . . Then when that letter came from
Miller—" Lance stopped. "Not *you*—Miller?"

How good to be able to talk. Lance is full of
loathing. I can see it. "Lance, think of it this way: Pop
and Miller were old men—sick—alone . . ."

He's *pleading* with me. "Good God, you're justify-ing murder."

Lance must understand. "They threatened my happiness—my home, my family—mine." His voice broke. No, no, I mustn't let myself get hysterical. Steady—my hand must be steady. "Now you know. You're the only one."

He raised the gun.

And to Lance, for the first time, came the icy shock of personal fear. This isn't Carl. This is a lunatic. He's going to kill me! I've got to *do* something. I'll jump him. No—he'll blow my head off before I can reach him. "You'll be heard."

Lance, Lance. "How many recognize the sound of a gun? Backfire."

"Someone'll see you leave!"

"I'll be careful."

"Carl, you can't do this!"

"I've got to."

"You're crazy!"

"No, boy—not now. Only once—"

Why'd he stop? There's something there. Please, God, please—let me hit it. "Sure you are! You've got to be insane to kill. Charlotte, Pop, Miller."

Miller . . . Can I tell him? Yes, I'll say it out loud. Then this too, this dark secret will be gone from me. "Lance, I'm going to tell you something." He heard his own breathing. "I was sane. I knew what I was doing—with her, with Pop. But with Miller . . . I went to Franklin to kill him. I knew that. But it was Charlotte I strangled. Do you understand? I don't remember killing Miller . . ."

I can't take much more. I'm no hero. I'm going to collapse. Lance felt the words jerk from him. "Of course you don't. You see? I was right. I told you."

No more of that. Carl felt a cold still peace. Now it will be over. "That won't happen again."

"Go ahead," panted Lance. "Okay—shoot. But get this: it *will* happen again. You'll come to one day and find you've killed Rose!"

What is he saying? *I?* Kill Rose? The boy's out of his mind.

"It's true, Carl. You've got the mark of the murderer. You killed Charlotte once—and again. And you'll go on killing her. And it will be Rose. One day she'll look at you—and you'll see Charlotte. She'll speak to you—and you'll hear Charlotte. And you'll kill her. And it will be Rose!"

The stabbing pain forked over Carl's eyes. Lance shouldn't shriek like that. He knows I'd give my life for Rose. I'll never go through *that* again. I was overwrought, excited. I'd never hurt Rose.

Lance's hands were lead. This is it! This is my chance—I've only got this split-second while he's off-guard. Why am I stuck to the floor? I've got to move. It's too late—it's too late!

Carl saw him. I shouldn't have relaxed. I've got to shoot! Lance—*don't!*

It didn't make much of a noise. Like backfire. Carl saw the gun still in his hand. He looked at it stupidly. He tried to lift it. Where was Lance?

He looked up—up—and saw Lance standing over him. Lance's eyes were black. Carl smiled. Poor Lance.

But he's standing. And I? I see everything so clear now.

I must tell him.

But this pain—it's killing me. *Rose—Rose*. Don't let me die.

Lance carried his story into the city room. The story was in his arms. He held it close to him, passed gaping faces, and laid Carl Chapman on the city desk, where he belonged.

"I've brought him home," Lance said. "He worked hard. All that counted was his wife and kids. She was a trespasser. Pop was a trespasser. Miller. I was a trespasser too. We wanted to take away his happiness. Look," he said, "there's a hole in his belly."

Someone pulled him by the arm. He turned obediently. Someone led him to a chair and sat him down.

"Lance, darling."

She had called him Lance. Why, it was Julie . . .

"Mr. McCleary," she said, "let's go out and get drunk."

"Yeah, Julie—let's go out and get drunk."

But he knew that no matter how much he drank, he could never get drunk enough.